OPERATOR 5:
ATTACK OF THE BLIZZARD MEN

SECRET SERVICE #5™

OPERATOR 5

AMERICA'S UNDERCOVER ACE

ATTACK OF THE
BLIZZARD MEN

By Curtis Steele

STEEGER BOOKS • 2020

CHAPTER 1
THE COMING OF THE COLD

I T WAS an hour destined to be recorded in the history of the United States in red letters of terror—that stifling August noon when a strange, sharp chill came creeping into the air of New York City, like the first breath of a silent and ghastly doom.

Until that fateful moment when the cold began to come, New York was sweltering in the hottest week of a torrid summer. A scorching sun, glaring out of a cloudless sky into the chasms of the city, converted the towering buildings into huge firebricks which multiplied the withering heat. Each breath, each movement of the suffering multitude in the metropolis was an effort. All New York strove to escape the oppressive humidity—until the cold began to come....

Hundreds of thousands had abandoned their homes and their offices and mobbed the beaches. Throngs struggled into every park in the dry, seeking relief. Every patch of shade was crowded, every window thrown wide to catch any stir of cooling wind; but even the shade was hot, and there was no breeze. A merciless, suffocating torridity pressed down upon the city. Then came the cold....

Silently it descended, swiftly, mysteriously, bringing horror, death and devastation.

Though the sun continued to glare, the heat diminished

each moment and an edged wind sprang up, bringing shivering discomfort to the scantily clad multitudes on the beaches. The puzzled throngs in the parks soon found the shade too cool and sought the warmth of the sun which, only a few moments ago, they had tried to avoid. But the sunlight was no longer warm. Windows closed before the rising, stinging wind. Heat gave way now to biting chill.

The cold had begun.

With it came widespread bewilderment, which rapidly changed to mounting fear of an unknown danger. Government meteorologists in their lofty observation stations peered, completely mystified, at the shrinking columns of their thermometers. This violent change in the weather was unprecedented, unpredicted, inexplicable. They could give no scientific reason to the clamoring newspapers for the sharpening chill which was spreading alarm throughout the city.

As the temperature plunged, crowds on beaches hastily abandoned their bathing suits in favor of street clothing. But the thin, summer garments offered only scant protection against a cold that was becoming steadily more acute. Great furnaces were hastily stoked to provide comfort to the millions shivering in chilled offices, apartments and theatres. Multitudes hastened to escape the streets, through which a cutting wind was now howling. A city which, only a few minutes before, had been desperately seeking relief from suffocating heat found itself unprepared to combat the piercing sting of midwinter weather!

Snow began to fall….

As fluttering white descended from the sky on this day in

August, obscuring the shine of the sun, a roadster hummed southward over the elevated highway flanking the Hudson River. Flakes plastered so thickly against the windshield that the clean-cut, brisk-mannered young man at the wheel was obliged to start the wiper. His clear eyes darkened with amazement. He carefully guided the powerful car over a roadbed now made treacherous by a growing layer of snow. Cold-bitten hands tight on the wheel, peering ahead through this blinding, August blizzard, he speeded on, as fast as he dared, upon a vital mission.

His name was James Christopher; in the secret archives of the United States Intelligence Service, he was designated Operator 5.

PEERING UP, as he descended a ramp, he saw that the high towers of the city's skyscrapers were obscured by the thickening storm. The cars and taxis which sped past him sheltered men, women and children clad only in light summer garments, shivering because of the sudden frigidity. The wind was piling drifts against the great pier of a Trans-Atlantic steamship line when Jimmy Christopher climbed hastily from his car. He fought against piercing blasts and choking snow, as he hurried down a long, broad lane of cement.

Customs officers, grimacing with the pain of the cold, scarcely glanced at the pass he held out as he hurried toward the gangplank of the gigantic steamer docked alongside the pier. Operator 5's watch told him that the sailing hour of the *Neptune*, one of the three largest and newest steamers in the world, was already past. Her mammoth funnels were almost obscured; her deserted promenades were covered with heaped whiteness.

A hand on his shoulder stopped Jimmy Christopher as he reached the deck, and he glanced around swiftly. The New Jersey shore had vanished in the swirling flakes. Fog-horns were hooting plaintively on the Hudson, but every other boat was enveloped and hidden by the storm. Nearby buildings were indicated only by faint spots of light shining through the fluttering veil of snow. A bright blanket of it lay packed on the shoulders and visored caps of the ship's officers who brought Operator 5 to a stop.

"Are you a passenger?" the man asked.

"I am not," Operator 5 replied tersely.

"It's past sailing time. No visitors can be admitted."

"It is absolutely necessary that I come aboard," Jimmy Christopher insisted—and his breath frosted in the air even as he spoke. He removed a green card from his pocket across which the red word PRESS was stamped, and displayed it "Is this sufficient?"

"It is not. We have special instructions."

A man in master's uniform, standing nearby, spoke now through the whine of the wind: "We sail at once—in spite of the storm." Another man, peering sharply at Operator 5, observed pointedly: "If you please, sir, the gang must be lowered now."

Jimmy Christopher, searching the cold-nipped, hard-lined face of the officers, demanded flatly: "You refuse absolutely to let me board the *Neptune!*"

"Absolutely!"

A wry smile played over Operator 5's lips as he turned back. He fought the biting wind as he went down; even as he left the gang, barked commands whipped the shivering pier crew into the task of lowering it. Racing to a stairway, plunging down it, he hurried across the loading dock, while snow whirled madly past him. The flying white concealed him as he hastened toward an open gate.

Giant hawsers were already being cast off. Two tugs were swinging their thickly padded prows against the gigantic *Neptune* while two others waited to guide her out into the Hudson. Though in a few moments she would begin to glide under her own power into the open sea, Operator 5 was still grimly determined to board her.

He peered through the swirling snow, detected a vague movement in the grayness, brought his fingers to his lips and whistled sharply. Swiftly, the shadow in the snow materialized as a small powerboat which shot toward the great pier. A boy huddled at its helm, braced against the tearing wind, shuddering with the bitter cold—but as he peered up at Operator 5 he grinned.

"Okay, Jimmy!" The words carried through the wailing of fog-horns and the gusting of the storm.

OPERATOR 5 lowered himself quickly; he dropped into the boat. It was his own; it had been shuttling back and forth here in the river at his orders, for use just in case of an emergency. Jimmy Christopher ordered the freckle-faced Irish lad at the wheel: "Alongside the *Neptune*, Tim!"

The great ship was a looming, black mass in the clouding

snow as Tim Donovan swerved the trim craft toward her. The plucky boy was Operator 5's unofficial assistant. Since the day two years previous when, on a drenching night on the lower East Side, he had saved Jimmy Christopher from a killer's bullet, they had worked side by side. A bond of affection and admiration held them together like blood brothers—bound them so strongly that no power but death would ever break it. Though he was too young to become an active member of the United States Intelligence, Tim's courage and resourcefulness had time and again justified Operator 5's reliance upon him. Now, he sent the little power-boat skimming across the waves toward the towering side of the *Neptune*.

The penetrating chill numbed the man and boy as they drifted close to the rearing wall of steel. Once the massive curve of the hull took them beyond sight of the tugs, Jimmy Christopher picked up a coil of stiff rope. Quickly, he inspected the grappling device spliced to one end. Straddling against the thrust of the icy wind, he threw the weighted end upward. It sailed into the snow-laden air—but a moment later, dropped back into the turgid water.

Twice more, as the monster of the sea backed into the Hudson, Operator 5 attempted to catch the hook on the unseen rail high above him. On the fourth attempt, he felt the impact and snap of the locking mechanism; he tested the rope, found it secure.

"Going up, Tim," Operator 5 announced tightly. "Stay alongside—wait for me. I think, when I come back—*if* I come back—we'll need to leave in a hurry!"

"Trust me, Jimmy!" the boy replied through chattering teeth.

Snow packed against the thin strand as Operator 5 climbed, making it slippery. Wind slapped at him viciously; his muscles ached with the cold and the strain of his effort as he pulled himself up. Gambling that the density of the swirling snow would hide him, he climbed hand over hand through interminable emptiness which was bitterly cold.

When, at last, the rail loomed within reach, he peered with stinging eyes across a deserted, snow-banked deck. While foghorns mourned, Operator 5 legged over the rail, pushed into the smoking-room. Inside, steam pipes were crackling and passengers huddling, but the faint warmth was inadequate protection against the fierce penetration of the cold.

Jimmy Christopher slapped snow from his clothing as he strode aft. Carefully, he peered ahead, alert to avoid being seen by any of the officers who had refused to admit him aboard.

Cautiously, he mounted the main companionway to the loftiest deck. At each landing he saw other passengers crowding about the steam pipes, wrapping themselves in blankets. Frosted windows shut out all view of either shore, but the penetrating cold seeped in relentlessly. Its sharp pinch brought pain to Jimmy Christopher's body as he strode to the entrance of the suite marked A—the largest, most costly on the boat....

OPERATOR 5'S knock stopped muffled voices which had been speaking inside. The door opened a crack; a wary eye peeked out. "What is it? What do you want?" an accented voice asked.

Operator 5 answered crisply: "This is the suite, is it not of

JIMMY CHRISTOPHER

the representatives of the Pan-National Peace Conference just concluded with the President of the United States?"

"Yes, yes, but—"

"I must see the representatives at once."

10

"It is impossible!"

"I am an agent of the United States Government"

"Impossible, I say!"

The blurted word snapped through as the door began to close. Operator 5's foot moved forward swiftly, into the crack. His shoulder slammed against it hard. The trained suppleness of his muscles overcame the frantic thrust that attempted to keep him out. He stepped across the threshold grimly, closing the door behind him, peering at the lean, white-faced man who confronted him indignantly.

Operator 5 recognized him at a glance, as well as the second chap who stood in the sumptuous stateroom—a short man, with bristling hair and a square face in which were two ominous, dark, deep-set eyes. The first was Ernesto Dupré, the second Karl Ould; both secretaries to representatives of European governments who had met with emissaries from every other nation of the globe, earlier this week in Washington.

This conclave of nations, called by the President of the United States, had been hailed by the world press as the greatest step

ever taken toward guaranteeing international peace. Solemnly, these famous statesmen had gathered to endorse a pact renouncing all aggressive militarism, pledging their governments to peaceful arbitration of all international disputes. Signed and sealed, the momentous treaty now lay in the archives of the Department of State in Washington; and today, many representatives of the participating governments were returning to their capitals.

The presence of these foreign statesmen on the *Neptune*, together with a vague clue he had unearthed earlier in the day had caused Operator 5 to board the departing vessel. Now his slight suspicions seemed partially confirmed.

"I am gratified to find myself so unwelcome," he said cuttingly to the enraged Dupré and Ould, "because I'm certain now I'm not mistaken."

He heard low voices beyond a connecting door, turned toward it quickly. Instantly Dupré rushed to block his way, and Ould darted to a position behind Operator 5. He came to a standstill between the two men, while the voices in the next room droned and the howling wind brought sharper chill into the air.

"Unless you leave at once—"

"I have no intention of leaving just yet, gentlemen," Operator 5 stated firmly. "I'm going into that room."

Two swift movements answered his statement Dupré' backed to the door, reached toward a weapon concealed in an armpit holster—the suspicious bulge of which Jimmy Christopher had already noted. Ould, behind Operator 5, made a similar threatening gesture. Swiftly, as their hands flashed, Jimmy Christopher bettered their speed.

He struck one swift blow to a point low on Dupré's neck. The lean man toppled stiffly against the wall; his hand, lifting with an automatic, stopped as if instantly frozen by the biting cold. Operator 5 whirled immediately upon Ould as a second weapon glinted upward. His hands clamped on Ould's wrist; his thumbs pressed hard at a vital nerve. Ould staggered away with a shrill squeal of dismay—and Jimmy Christopher sidestepped, the second gun in his hands.

INSTANTLY, OULD leaped. Operator 5 dropped the automatic into his pocket as he wrenched aside—but hard hands clamped on his throat and sharp fingernails dug deep. The savage attack jolted Jimmy Christopher backward. Because the necessity of raising no alarm made use of his gun impossible, he struggled desperately to launch an Oriental counter-attack. He wrapped one arm hard around Ould's neck, pulled the other forcibly against the small of his assailant's back. His tempered muscles strained as he strove to bend Ould back and away.

A sharp click of displaced vertebrae—a swift intake of breath—and the hands crushing Jimmy Christopher's throat fell limp. Unconsciousness spilled the short man to the floor. Operator 5 stepped away from his body alertly, peered grimly at the lean man who was still propped against the closed door, as powerless to move as a statue. Jimmy Christopher carried the rigid man to a bed, snapped the Luger snugly into his hand, and faced the door through which low, mumbling voices could still be heard.

Brilliantly executed jiu-jitsu tactics had rendered both Dupré and Ould strength-less, but Operator 5 knew his familiarity with Oriental tactics, would be useless once he stepped through the door in front of him….

He holstered his automatic; suddenly stepped through, backed to the closed door, and faced the twelve men who were gathered around a table.

His glance flashed swiftly from man to man. Each he recognized as a representative of a world power, men who, only a few days previously, had conferred with the President of the United States. Each face he saw now was filled with dismay. He glimpsed, on the table, a vellum document bearing red wax seals and red ribbons. A bearded statesman held his pen-hand poised, ready to place his signature at the bottom of a long column of names.

Jimmy Christopher stepped forward quickly. The dignitaries at the table jerked to their feet, uttering startled exclamations, as he reached toward the sealed document. Other hands snatched too, but his move was swiftest. He backed away, fingers tight on the heavy pages, a grim smile curving his lips. The nearest of the men advanced with quick, threatening steps as Operator 5 observed in a crackling tone: "The United States government wishes to inspect this treaty, gentlemen!"

He jerked open the door, lurched out as a husky voice blurted: "Stop him! In God's name, stop him!" He shot a bolt into its socket as the knob rattled and heavy fists hammered the panels. Darting across the room where Dupré and Ould still lay unconscious, he shouldered out. A voice was shouting frantically into the ship's telephone: "Captain Thaler at once—*at once!*" when Operator 5 dashed away....

HE PAUSED at the head of a companionway to glance swiftly at the imposing document He saw phrases that quickened his heart and filled him with dread. *In the event of hostilities with the government of the United States, of whatever cause....* Hurrying steps behind him, alarmed voices, caused him to thrust the treaty inside his coat and plunge downward. The telephonic alarm, he knew, was already starting ship's officers in a manhunt for him. He raced breathlessly to the deck where he had boarded the *Neptune*.

Thrusting out into blinding snow and the cold of a punishing wind, he sprang across mounded white. As he climbed over the rail where the grappling hook was caught, a shot cracked and a bullet screamed through the storm. Operator 5 glimpsed several armed officers charging toward him as he gripped the rope and plummeted downward.

Wind howled around him; flying snow choked him, as he dangled on the stinging strand. Again a gun barked. Heart racing, he saw the powerboat nosing through the snow toward him. Tim Donovan, shuddering with the bitter cold, seized his arm to guide him into the bobbing boat. Twice more, revolvers cracked through the fury of the storm and bullets whined past Operator 5 as he hurled himself toward the helm.

Jimmy Christopher jerked the throttle wide. He crouched beside Tim Donovan in deep-piled snow as the boat traced a long, swift wake across the icy water. Their speed sharpened the edge of the wind as they shot out into the storm-torn river. The *Neptune* faded into a gigantic shadow, as devastating chill spread over all New York.

Streets and avenues which, an hour ago, had been blistering with summer heat were now deserted to the howling arctic blasts and piled high with drifts of white. Tall spires were shrouded in an icy mantle which caused relentless frigidity to seep through every frosted window. Hundreds of thousands of automobiles, busses, trucks, and trolleys were snowbound. Millions had attempted to escape the storm indoors, but the cold pursued them grimly, like an implacable foe. The few men and women who struggled afoot through mounting drifts to reach their homes were inviting the death that had already overtaken those stiff, hoary figures lying motionless under dune-like snow banks….

Thermometers had already dropped far below the zero point, and still the polar blasts grew more intense. Upon this scene of white havoc, a sun looked down—a sun which no longer radiated the faintest warmth. The cold had come!

CHAPTER 2
THE ARMY OF
THE ABSOLUTE ZERO

THE SNOW stopped—stopped not because warmth was returning to an icebound area, but because that bitter chill had sent every particle of moisture spilling frozen from the air. The cold did not abate—instead, it settled steadily into a stronger, more crushing force. The wind howled itself away, and a deadly quiet followed. The power of the cold maintained its grip with deadly silence....

Into the East River—a swollen chaos of chunked ice—Operator 5's speedboat shuttled. Numbed, almost unable to move, Jimmy Christopher and Tim Donovan huddled in the feeble warmth generated by the engine. They peered landward along streets drifted high with snow—at rearing skyscrapers which had become windowless, white towers—as they fought their way toward the boat-house in which Operator 5 kept his craft.

Frozen into silence by the relentless cold, they swerved to the little pier. They dragged themselves up stiffly, made the boat fast with numb hands, and ran toward a door at the rear of the structure. Into the small room beyond, walled with cupboards—a place which Operator 5 maintained as an emergency base—the cold penetrated with the same paralyzing force. Desperately they drew heavy coats from closets and pulled into them.

Jimmy Christopher thrust paper and kindling into the iron stove in the corner. They watched eagerly as the first feeble blaze crackled from the wood. Yet, as they huddled near, starving

17

for warmth, they scarcely felt it. Operator 5 noted that the fire started with curious slowness, as though the arctic temperature were too powerful for it to combat.

Tim Donovan gasped shuddering: "Golly, it's cold! It's colder now than I ever remember it—even in winter. Nothing like this ever happened before, did it, Jimmy?"

"Never, Tim," Operator 5 answered tightly. He was peering at a thermometer on the wall. "It's twenty below zero now—and still dropping fast. But regardless of that, Tim, we've got to get to Washington as fast as—"

He broke off, listening to a sudden, loud sound which snarled through the walls of the little building. It was a combined clanking and snorting—as though a huge machine had abruptly gone into action. The grinding noise pulled Operator 5, curious, from the fire; bundling his coat around him against the penetrating chill of the air, he opened a side door. His exclamation of dismay brought Tim Donovan anxiously to his side. They peered together along the snow-banked street.

In one whitened wall, a pair of broad doors had opened disclosing the black interior of a garage. Beyond the heap of whiteness which still blocked it, moving figures were visible. With Tim Donovan at his shoulder, Jimmy Christopher gazed astounded at creatures who seemed to have materialized from an age long past—men clad in suits of mail!

In shining helmets and glittering tunics, they worked feverishly at some mysterious task. Their garments, Operator 5 saw, were covered with small leaves of metal which overlapped like fish-scales. The same material covered their heads completely, and they looked out of their hoods through huge, goggle-like lenses. Though the cold stabbed bitterly at Operator 5 and Tim Donovan as they watched, these strangely clad men moved with a freedom which indicated they did not feel the deadly, sub-zero temperature at all!

AS JIMMY CHRISTOPHER drew back alertly, closing the door until only a crack remained, the rumbling noise inside the garage grew louder. Cold sunlight glinted on the conical metallic superstructure of a vehicle which crawled into the street. It headed straight at the snow-bank, and suddenly the mound of white was heaved upward. It spilled aside, revealing a steel monster crawling on caterpillar treads into the drifted street.

"A tank!" Tim Donovan blurted.

The tank breasted the snow with ease, spun, and began clattering along the street. It cleared its own way, advanced with amazing speed toward the center of the city. Behind it, as it moved, whole squads of the strangely clad men appeared. Garbed in gleaming metal, turning weird, goggled eyes smartly forward, each armed with holstered revolver and shouldered rifle, they swung into trim formation behind the tank with a brisk dispatch which revealed discipline and a well-planned stratagem.

Operator 5 drew back in alarm; about to close the door, he paused. Nearby streets seemed to echo the sound of the crawling tank as it vanished from sight, but Operator 5 realized instantly that these additional noises were not echoes. He became certain of it as he listened; his face grew white. He bolted the door, turned stiffly, and found Tim Donovan peering at him in wide-eyed wonder.

"Other tanks are going into action all around us!" Jimmy Christopher blurted. "It may be happening all over the city—scores, even hundreds of hidden tanks advancing at once—with thousands of men behind them!"

"But that wasn't a United States tank, Jimmy!" Tim declared, aghast "And they can't be United States army men!"

"You're right, Tim—they're not. It means—"

Again Operator 5 broke off, choked with astonishment. The dull concussion which shook the air silenced him, brought a deeper whiteness to his drawn face. Muffled echoes rolled through the bitter air, seemed to shake even the frozen ground. Again he opened the door and peered out, when three more explosions blasted—one so violently that Operator 5 spun to turn stinging eyes across the ice-caked river.

Flame flashed high from the turgid stream, vanishing instantly, leaving a rolling cloud of smoke drifting over the water. As the haze moved, dim outlines became visible through it. The outline of a boat appeared; and, as the air cleared, Operator 5 recognized the craft as a Coast Guard cutter! He saw it list heavily, even as terrorized men rushed across its deck to escape the inevitable plunge to the bottom.

The terrific concussion had cleaved the craft nearly in two. It was a broken, doomed thing as it swiftly wallowed deeper into the water. The crew sprang desperately over the rail as Operator 5 watched. With a sharper cold striking his heart than that in the air, he saw them plunge into the icy water, knew they were doomed to a freezing death the instant they reached the wind-swept shore.

Operator 5 hurried from the door, stumbling through waist-deep snow, as Tim Donovan struggled behind him. A broader view of the river was revealed to them after they fought their way to the end of the street. In the spreading whiteness, they glimpsed movement which held their anxious attention. Wet, black metal gleamed in the cold sunlight—a sleek, rounded hump, the superstructure of a submarine!

"That boat was torpedoed!" Tim Donovan exclaimed.*

Operator 5 blurted: "Back, Tim! There's a machine-gun—"

---

* AUTHOR'S NOTE: An "invisible" torpedo, propelled by electricity instead of compressed air and fired by invisible means, has been adopted for German submarines, according to the *London Daily Telegraph*. Both improvements, says the *Telegraph's* naval correspondent, will make submarine attacks on merchantmen of slow or moderate speed much more deadly, although to fast warships the torpedoes may not be so dangerous as the old type.

Electric propulsion eliminates the tell-tale trail of bubbles which always accompanies the compressed air type. The discharge has been made invisible by a device that cuts off the air blast the moment the torpedo leaves the submarine tube. Normally, the discharge of a torpedo from a submarine is betrayed by an upheaval on the surface of the ocean.

The *Telegraph* asserts Germany's submarine experiments have been conducted in defiance of the peace treaty embargo through the collaboration of "certain neutral countries."

"These tests," it asserts, "are related not only to new weapons but to new methods of construction, like the Flamm superstability hull, which, it is claimed, enables a boat so built to carry twice the weight in armament and protection carried by the conventional submarine of the same tonnage."

A SHARP, staccato stutter interrupted him—the swift *brrrt!* of the gun he had glimpsed. Slugs screamed across the water; lines of deep, small holes smacked into the bank beside Operator 5 even as he uttered the warning. He leaped aside, tugging Tim Donovan's arm, and together they sprawled into the soft whiteness of the snow as the bullets whined waspishly above them. For a long moment as they lay half-buried in the cold stuff—which could not protect, but rather, trapped them—the tattoo from the submarine continued.

Operator 5 sprang up the instant the snapping reports ceased. He rushed, with Tim Donovan, toward the open door of the pier-house. Again the gun stuttered; and from farther away, another echoed its burst, and still another. Jimmy Christopher, closing the door, safely out of range of the submarine's gun, peered toward the far corner to see another tank clanking past and men in suits of mail running at its side. He slapped the door shut, blurted: "Invasion!"

The chorus of ominous sounds which penetrated the walls verified his conclusion: the spitting of machine-guns from scattered points, thundering explosions which meant devastation from other torpedoes, the clanking of mighty tanks as they crawled, the muffled tread of marching men in the street....

"The gyro, Tim!"

In the urgency of that moment, both Jimmy Christopher and the boy almost forgot the bitter cold that attacked them. They struggled against its stiffening force as they mounted a short flight of stairs. The room into which they stumbled was large and square—empty save for an autogyro standing at one side. Operator 5 hastened toward it, ordered the boy breathlessly: "Draw the roof!" He climbed to the crank, pumped the cylinders of the engine full of fuel, made contact.

Operator 5 kept the gyro hidden in this secret hangar for any emergency that might arise; he took great pains to keep the power-plant in perfect condition. Yet now he struggled against a handicap he could not have foreseen—penetrating cold which thickened the motor oil and kept the fuel from igniting. Again and again, he wrenched the crank, fruitlessly, while Tim Donovan labored in a corner of the room.

The boy was likewise fighting the effect of the cold on the mechanism used to withdraw the roof. He had operated it on previous occasions with the utmost ease; but now, the oil on the bearings was sticky and the grease in the gears almost frozen. With all his strength, Tim Donovan strove to turn that crank; and, little by little, painfully, the white sky appeared—the frigid sunshine streamed in—while Operator 5 battled to start the gyro's motor.

The engine sneezed, turned over, stopped; it coughed again, held a moment, stopped again. Desperately, Operator 5 worked until, at last, a burst of power came which smoothed off and held. Alertly, he adjusted the mixture to compensate for the coldness and played the throttle. His face was lined with anxiety, blue with the bitter cold, as Tim Donovan turned from the other crank and clambered into the pit his task finally completed.

"Jimmy! The guns in the river—"

"We'll have to risk them, Tim!" Operator 5 grated. "We've got to get to Washington as fast as we can! Take the controls, old timer!"

JIMMY CHRISTOPHER twisted to the craft's short-wave equipment as the boy obeyed. Punishing as the Arctic temperature was, they almost forgot it in their anxious wait for the engine and the radio tubes to warm. With an icy handset held in one gloved—but numb—hand, Operator 5 at last heard the hiss of the installation. With the oscillator trimmed, he spoke urgently into the microphone:

"Calling TS-NY! Calling TS-NY!"

The designation was that of the Manhattan headquarters of the United States Intelligence where men were always on duty at the bank of radio receivers. Yet no immediate answer came. Jimmy Christopher waited tensely. Hearing Tim play the throttle easily, he commanded: "Take her up!" The craft was already moving when Operator 5 called his signal again: "TS-NY! TS-NY!"

The gyro rolled a short distance across the smooth floor; and abruptly it lifted! Of the latest design, capable of soaring almost vertically, with practically no take-off run, it surged through the open roof with its weird vanes spinning. The drone of the propellers beat the air powerfully as it lifted above the surrounding buildings. Deftly, exercising all the skilled training Jimmy Christopher had given him, the tough lad sent the craft into a

24

swift climb while Operator 5 huddled in the biting wind and signaled again:

"Calling TS-NY! Calling—"

"TS-NY on your wave!"

The sharp chatter of a machine-gun almost blanketed the response from Operator 5's ears. In dismay, he jerked around to peer over the cowling. Lying in the white-spotted band of the East River, he saw the sleek blackness of the submarine. On its superstructure, men clad in the same, strange, metal garments were crouching over the machine-gun. Its barrel was aiming directly toward the swerving gyro, hurling leaden death into the air, as Tim Donovan desperately strove to elude the onslaught.

"In-shore, Tim!" Jimmy Christopher gasped. "Get behind the buildings! Watch that water as you climb!"

A long, withering burst from the machine-gun sought the flitting gyro as its target as Tim Donovan maneuvered hastily. Slugs whined through the crisp air, sent vibrations through the craft as they pierced the tail. Operator 5 huddled low as the boy swerved out of range of the murderous attackers. The hail of bullets stopped and the gyro sped northward; and again Jimmy Christopher heard the answering call of TS-NY.

"On your wave!"

"Operator 5 speaking from Mobile PG. Connect me with W-8!"

The voice at TS-NY answered rapidly: "W-8 is at the telephone now, flashing urgent information to Z-7 at WDC-13. He cannot leave his post, Operator 5!"

TIM DONOVAN

Jimmy Christopher urged: "Please cut me in on that conversation!"

Electrical clicks echoed over the air while intricate connec-

tions were made which would enable Operator 5, soaring over arctic New York, to listen in on the long-distance telephone conversation with the central Intelligence headquarters in Washington. He peered down and saw, in the snow-banked streets and ice-caked rivers, an amazing panorama of invasion....
IN THE white chasms of the city, Jimmy Christopher spotted scores of speeding tanks—corps of metal monsters driving toward strategic positions. With them went squad after squad of armed men, clad in coveralls and hoods of bright, metal scales. The penetrating cold made resistance to their advance virtually impossible as they swarmed the icy thoroughfares of the city— taking command!

In the ice-flecked water which completely surrounded Manhattan, a score of shiny-backed submarines were floating, each with a mailed crew stationed at machine-guns. The weapons blasted slugs at any moving craft and along the waterfront streets. At the great docks in the Hudson, and in Brooklyn, steamers were listing and sinking at their piers, rammed by torpedoes, while thickening ice surrounded them. In that

isolating circle of water, the war-whales had assumed positions of crushing power.

Up from the dark depths of the sea, and out of the gloom of hidden barracks, the submarine tanks and the mailed troops had swarmed, striking a devastating blow against a city paralyzed by ravaging, cosmic cold.

Operator 5 soared high above the helpless metropolis, with the plucky Irish lad at the controls of the gyro, and watched in dismay the spreading power of invasion. Abruptly, voices sang out of the bitter emptiness of the ether.

First, the rushing voice of W-8, speaking over the special long-distance line with central Intelligence headquarters WDC-13 in Washington: "Reports are coming in erratically, Chief. Something is wrong with the wires. It must be the cold—for it's forty below at least, with the mercury frozen in the thermometer bulb here. Can you hear me, Chief?"

The throaty voice which answered was that of a man known only as Z-7—even to his most trusted Intelligence agents—the commander-in-chief of the far-flung undercover organization: "I can't understand that, W-8. Washington has experienced no such storm. I can scarcely hear you, but—the reports, man! What the devil is happening in New York?"

"It's invasion—nothing else can explain it—but I have only the most fragmentary reports. My men in the field are trapped by this damnable cold. We know that armed men are taking command of key points in the city, while we're helpless to stop them. But we can't identify the enemy. We're doing our best, but this is work for the Army and Navy!"

Z-7's chesty voice answered swiftly: "I'll speak with the President and the Chief of Staff now. Keep reports flashing to me, W-8. At all costs, in spite of every handicap, keep your headquarters functioning—do everything possible to keep its location a secret from the invading force!"

"I can scarcely hear you, Z-7! The cold is putting the line out of commission!"

Even as Operator 5 listened, he heard the two voices fade into emptiness. His wireless equipment was also affected by the crippling cold. Abandoning the handset, he sensed that the motor of the gyro was functioning sluggishly, as though it could not effect combustion against the powerful frigidity. Tim Donovan yielded the controls to him as they whisked through a blank white sky, through heat-less sunshine.

Beneath the flitting, vaned craft, the organized invasion functioned smoothly in spite of the bitter cold.

TOWARD POLICE Headquarters on Centre Street crawled four snarling tanks, flanked by platoons of mailed troops. They charged into the building where hundreds of men were struggling to stave off the paralyzing effects of the cold. Guns leveled, eyes peering through their goggles, the mailed men moved briskly, alertly, past dead policemen who lay frozen stiff in the corridors. On those hardy few who tried to resist their advance, they turned their machine-guns. The staccato reports echoed throughout the building as the invaders assumed control.

They swept into the radio broadcasting-room where men lay frozen, and took charge. They seized the telephone switchboards. They confiscated all guns, ammunition and tear-gas bombs.

Their withering attacks forced a few remaining officers into the frigid streets, where death was certain to claim them. None but the mailed men remained alive inside that great building after the first few minutes of the well planned attack. Police Headquarters became a fort controlled by an unknown enemy.

Each precinct station, each firehouse, saw a repetition of the carnage. Every stronghold fell before the advancing mailed men. Their power spread swiftly from the Central Post Office to each branch. They swooped upon banks where men and women lay already dead of the freezing death, and relentlessly took charge. They swept into telephone exchanges, and telegraph offices. Armored hordes flooded the broadcasting stations which the cold had now stilled. They swarmed into every electrical power plant within the metropolis and their guns won swift victories in each. Scores of them stormed into deserted newspaper offices, controlling the wires and the presses. Grand Central Terminal and Pennsylvania Station—as well as all bus depots, ferry houses, and bridges—fell to their power. Over all these strategic points, their power descended like a merciless paralysis—while the mailed men moved forward, seemingly oblivious of an Arctic coldness which killed.

At points beyond the limits of New York City, the terrifying power of the invaders struck. At Fort Hancock, on Sandy Hook, where giant guns guarded New York Harbor, the cold had taken its hoary toll. Powerless against such silent force, lacking orders from Washington, men and officers perished in the inflexible frost At Fort Totten, the polar temperatures had slain like a white plague. On Mitchell Field, Long Island, planes and hangars lay buried under heaped snow. Flying was impossible—impossible not only because engines could not be started, but because almost all officers and pilots had perished in the storm.

With amazing speed, the giant war-machine of the enemy seized upon the helpless city. No report of the invasion could escape the metropolis once the mailed troops closed down. It became a city of cold silence, unreachable by wire or radio, impenetrable to train, bus, automobile or airplane. The invading force, aided by the bitter cold, erected impassable barriers around and above it After the crushing polar temperature closed upon the city, only one craft succeeded in escaping the invisible trap—the autogyro of Operator 5...!

FLYING HIGH under a frigid sun, coaxing the power-plant along, Jimmy Christopher navigated southward through the cold. And as he sped, that very cold began to disappear. From his high vantage point, he noted white boundaries beyond which the storm bad not struck. He felt again the warmth of the sunlight, saw again the green of summer in the landscape below. The ice and snow had vanished! In amazement Operator 5 noted the swift change as he urged his craft toward Washington at top speed....

CHAPTER 3
STORM OVER WASHINGTON

A GRAVE man sat tensely at his desk in the study of the White House. The President of the United States had put aside all routine affairs of government to confer with the two men who confronted him now. He had said little since their hasty arrival; he listened intently as they spoke. They were his chief lieutenants in two highly important agencies of the United States—Major-General Falk, Chief of Staff of the Joint Board of the Army and Navy, and Z-7, commander of the Intelligence.

"I can't reach New York at all, Mr. President!" General Falk blurted. "It's impossible to contact Fort Hancock or Fort Totten or Governor's Island or Mitchell Field by telephone, telegraph or wireless. We don't know what's happened in New York, and we can't learn!"

Z-7 declared: "It's equally impossible to raise TS-NY. That office is exceedingly well-hidden. I'm sure it hasn't been seized. Our telephone and telegraph lines should still be operating—but they're not I'm able to connect instantly with every sub-headquarters in the country—except New York."

The Chief Executive, solemnly studying the drawn face of the Chief of Staff, asked: "It's certain, then, that virtually all means of communication and transportation have been seized by this mysterious enemy? Our military strength in that area is no strength at all. Our only means of reclaiming the city is to drive an armed force into it from outside the enemy lines."

The three men in the study fully realized the perilous situation in which they were placed. The fragmentary reports leaking out of the doomed city had mentioned submarines in rivers and bay, but had revealed that the real strength of the invaders lay in man-power—the troops and tanks now dominating the island city.*

To send the Navy's Scout Squadron into the Bay with orders to turn their guns on the city would mean killing thousands of citizens. To hurl shells crashing into the Army Posts, which had become strongholds of the enemy, would mean destroying those vital units of defense. To order bombing planes into the city for the purpose of driving the invaders out would likewise mean the slaughter of American non-combatants—the very people who must be protected. As they gazed at each other in silence, the President, the Chief of Staff and Z-7 found themselves faced with a predicament demanding the most careful strategy.

"We must," General Falk declared firmly, "limit our area of attack. Orders to the Scout Squadron must concentrate on

---

* AUTHOR'S NOTE: The danger of the American position is shown by the following statement by Lieut-General Von Metzsch, a military expert of international reputation who, during the World War, held various important posts with the German General Staff:

"If a belligerent succeeds in establishing a suitable base of operations in the enemy's country, he can then systematically proceed with his own war organization with no danger of enemy attacks, unless it be from the air. On the other hand, the country that is attacked will find all attempts at organization for war crippled by the loss of important vital centers of supplies. To a certain extent, provision will have to be made to compensate for these losses, but it may be assumed that the limits of such compensation will quickly be reached, whereas the enemy invading the country will have been able to increase his war strength."

sinking submarines and no more—and even that is a dangerous risk. The Air Corps will cooperate in that attempt, but there, too, their objective is limited to the water. This leaves a drive into the city by our Army as the only possible move remaining."

"With all means of transportation in and out of the city in the hands of the invaders," the President added, "your attack must concentrate on the bridges. The Holland Tunnel may provide a means of entry. A few ferries still remaining on the Jersey and Brooklyn sides of the rivers may be an additional aid. Yet—"

"It's a problem we must solve on the scene," the Chief of Staff answered. "If I have your orders, sir—"

"Keeping in mind," the President continued, "that our counter-attack must spare the lives of our civilians, your orders are to retake New York as soon as possible."

"Yes, sir!"

THE CHIEF OF STAFF saluted smartly, about-faced, and strode from the study. The few brief sentences exchanged between the Chief Executive and him were sufficient to marshal the nation's defense. Within a few moments, the gigantic organisms of Both Army and Navy must begin to function, even though under staggering handicaps. Gravely the President gazed at the closed door during a silent moment, then turned to Z-7.

"At this moment," he said, "your Intelligence force in the New York area is helpless. It is as though we have no sub-headquarters there at all. Therefore it is absolutely necessary that we establish communication with the Manhattan unit."

Z-7 smiled grimly. "New York City has become the same as a foreign territory with which we are at war. It means sending men, as spies, through armed lines. It calls for my most capable men, Mr. President Operator 5 is my best agent—he is my choice for the task of opening the way. As soon as he arrives—"

Z-7 broke off, listening to a muffled drumming sound in the air. It was the exhaust of an aircraft hovering low and coming lower. It turned the chief of the Intelligence toward the study door, brought a grave smile of satisfaction to the lips of the President.

"Operator 5 is here now."

Z-7 hurried from the study, out the East entrance of the White House. As he hurried across the dark lawn, he was followed by members of the special detail of the Secret Service charged with protecting the President. Warily, they peered up at the weird varied craft which was swinging down. Z-7 ran toward it as its fat tires touched, as its vanes drooped and its power-plant whirred off.

Jimmy Christopher dropped from the pit with Tim Donovan. Their heavy coats and gloves were discarded now, for sharply contrasting with the deadly frigidity of New York, the weather in Washington was oppressively warm.

"The President has just ordered a counter-attack upon New York, Operator 5," the chief declared, as they hurried toward the White House. "It's a ticklish situation. Have you any information which would help?"

"None, Chief," Jimmy Christopher answered as he entered the corridor. "I tried constantly, while flying toward Washington, to reach TS-NY by radio, but I couldn't. The attack was planned in every minute detail, and functioned like clockwork. Whoever our enemy may be, the command is as shrewd as it is daring. Every element is telling against us—surprise and an unparalleled genius for military coördination."

As Z-7 seized the knob of the President's study he asked in bewilderment: "But what is the real plan behind all this? My reports show that the enemy has attacked only a few points outside the city. They have seized New York and scarcely anything more, though the way lies open to them. Is it possible they intend to hold their present position without attempting to penetrate inland?"

"They've taken control of the financial center of the nation, chief," Jimmy Christopher pointed out. "That was their first objective. As for die next attack in this master plan—"

" 'The next!' " Z-7 exclaimed. "What the devil are you hinting, Operator 5?"

THE DOOR was open. Jimmy Christopher answered the

36

chief's question with only cryptic silence as he strode toward the President's desk. His hand clasped the Chief Executive's. On the blotter, a communication was lying which had been received at the White House during Operator 5's swift flight to the Capital. Indicating it, the President asked:

"I have been waiting for an explanation of this information, Operator 5. What does it mean?"

The few terse lines read:

> I am bringing to the White Hone documentary proof that the attack on New York City is the remit of a cabal among certain world powers.
>
> Operator 5.

Jimmy Christopher reached inside his coat and, from a cleverly concealed pocket, removed the thick folder of vellum pages he had seized aboard the *Neptune*. He opened it showing the imposing signatures and the red seals, and spoke rapidly.

"Mr. President, this document bears the names of the statesmen who only a few days ago met with you here, in the White House, to sign a pact of peace. That agreement has now become a meaningless scrap of paper. Those statesmen were promising peace while they were actually fomenting war. The invasion of New York is part of their plan—and this document is a treaty of the alliance of world powers behind the attack."

The President stared. "Do you mean that the invasion of New York is not the act of a single nation, but of a secret entente?"

"I do. This treaty is an appalling document, but there is no doubt whatsoever as to its authenticity. I actually saw the last

signature being placed on it. Here, sir, is an international agreement between a dozen world powers concerning the division
of spoils, once the United States is subjugated!"

The President took the document in his hands, gazed aghast
at the signatures. He saw before him an attested statement
which proved that the war-power of the world was marshaled
against the United States—a vast military machine, unequaled
in world history.

"That treaty, Mr. President," Operator 5 hurried on, "embod-
ies no explanation for victimizing the United States—but the
motive isn't hard to find. There is one thing which binds all the
signatory nations together. Traditional enemies sat at the same
conference table to create that document because they all are
haunted by the same dread—fear of the tremendous shift of
advantage and power which will occur when this country enters
the next war, as it inevitably must."

Peering up, the President asked huskily: "Operator 5, how
did you learn of the existence of this treaty?"

Jimmy Christopher explained rapidly. While the representatives of the world powers were gathered in Washington, to
sign the President's peace pact, Z-7's orders had detailed him
to watch the members of the conclave. Washington had buzzed
like a hive during the momentous deliberations, with numer-
ous conferences held to decide upon the terms. Operator 5's
suspicions had been aroused by the unusual precautions against
observation taken by one of the groups.

"I found," he explained, "that the Quadruple Alliance was
holding important meetings in secret. They were exchanging

messages by secret messenger with the Asiatic Entente. I knew it might involve grave consequences, but I risked intercepting one of these messages."

HE HAD found, he added, that it was couched in a code which was one of the most difficult in the world to decipher. The very complexity of the system of secret communication had strengthened his suspicions that an international project of vast importance was being deliberated. It was not until the adjournment of the peace negotiations that he had succeeded in discovering the key to the message.

"It stated that the terms of an unnamed treaty were now agreed on. It stipulated a meeting to be held in New York at a designated place. A name appearing in it—that of Commissar Evol Kran, the most dangerous militarist in the world today—forced me to conclude that the treaty could not possibly comply with the peace pact. The sentence which urged me to investigate, Mr. President, was Commissar Kran's plan of attack will be put into execution immediately the treaty is signed."

Z-7 blurted: "Then Kran's evil genius must be behind the invasion of New York!"

"Kran," Operator 5 agreed, "is imbued with ambitions of conquest more daring today than Genghis Khan, Caesar or Napoleon in their times. It is literally true that the powers of the world have ganged together to subjugate the United States under Commissar Kran—and this signed treaty is proof of it."

The President's face had gone white. He sank into his chair and stared at the document. There was a moment of silence, while a breeze stirred the curtains on the open windows of the study. Stunned by Operator 5's revelation, the Chief Executive sat motionless.

Operator 5's eyes had sharpened; his manner had become wary. He searched the President's face, and that of Z-7, during the silent interval. Both men were intent upon the appalling situation revealed by the secret treaty; they were scarcely aware of their surroundings. A grim expectancy tightened Operator 5's mouth as he spoke:

"Though I succeeded in getting hold of a copy of the treaty, Mr. President, it still exists as an active agreement among the world powers who are bent on eliminating us from the international situation."

Gravely the President declared: "This treaty actually creates a super-nation—founded as an enemy of the United States—an enemy that has already struck without the formality of declaring war. If we succeed in driving the invaders out of New York, this agreement will turn all the armed power of the world against us. How can we possibly hope for victory against such a tremendous foe?"

"I believe, sir," Operator 5 said quietly, "that our defense will find itself faced with a far greater task than merely reclaiming New York."

The President's startled eyes widened. "What do you mean?" he asked quickly. Operator 5 was about to speak when a knock sounded on the door. The President's call brought his secretary into the room. With a murmur of apology, the secretary stepped beyond the desk and closed the windows.

"The weather is turning very cool, sir," he said.

Dismayed realization came into the President's eyes. Z-7 grew pale as he gazed at Jimmy Christopher. They did not speak until the secretary had withdrawn. Then the Washington chief blurted:

"Is that what you mean—the cold?"

"The cold," Operator 5 answered quietly. "The storm that hit New York was not a meteorological freak. It was man-made. Gentlemen, it is some new and terrible weapon of war. It opened the way for an invasion of New York. It is striking at Washington now!"

Even as Operator 5 spoke, the sharpness in the air increased perceptibly. Gazing through the window, the President and Z-7 saw men and women hurrying along Pennsylvania Avenue, whipped by a keen-edged wind. The warmth of the summer sun was rapidly yielding to the penetrating blasts which came swooping from an ominous sky with growing violence. The wintry chill, reaching into the President's study through closed windows, brought with it a shudder of discomfort and dread.

"The cold," Operator 5 declared grimly, "is coming. The cold, Mr. President—and the enemy!"

THE COLD came to Washington with relentless swiftness. As though pouring from the gelid depths of cosmic space, it struck the hub of the nation with terrifying death and devastation.

Short minutes ago, newsboys had been shouting startling headlines on the corners.

New York Paralyzed by Terrific Storm!
Thousands Dead in Crippled City!
Armed Men Swarm City!
Cold Takes Heavy Toll!
New York Isolated by Storm Invaders!

Those cries were a tocsin of terror. Now the same cold descended upon Washington, out of a frigid sky, like the icy breath of a dreadful doom.

Shivering thousands hurried along the wind-torn streets in a mad scramble to escape the penetrating chill. Walls could not hold out the piercing cold which stole silently into every home and office. Those who fled the thoroughfares, in a desperate endeavor to find shelter, found instead that there was no possible escape from the frigidity. Thousands of furnaces were fired; yet their warmth was scant protection against the lowering temperature. The grip of the silent, invisible death grew tighter with every passing moment....

Snow fell. It materialized in the cold sky as if by magic Swirling on the polar winds, it became blindingly thick within a few moments. Pavements which, a short time ago, had been sizzling under the glare of a blazing sun now were carpets of white—while the same sun shone, devoid of heat. Howling blasts packed the flakes against curbs and buildings. The dome of the Capitol became white as a sepulcher; the towering needle of the Washington Monument like a giant tombstone in the wintry storm. Arctic fury descended upon the seat of the nation's government with cataclysmic violence.

The cold had come.

In the historic study in the White House, the President sat tensely at his desk, a chilled telephone receiver pressed to his ear. The air had become piercingly sharp, and each moment was making the sting of the cold more painful. Even as he watched, amazed, the Chief Executive had seen celebrated Pennsylvania Avenue utterly transformed. Wind howled savagely past the whitening windows as the President spoke imperatively over the line.

"General Falk! Your plan to counterattack New York must be abandoned. There is every reason to believe that invading troops will swarm into Washington under cover of this deadly cold. They must be met and repulsed at all costs. Those are your orders, General Falk!"

Operator 5 strode swiftly out the study door as the President rose. Tim Donovan was waiting in the corridor. The boy was shivering. The White House Secret Service detail were tramping back and forth in an energetic effort to warm themselves. The Irish lad hurried to Jimmy Christopher's side and heard through the shrieking of the arctic blasts:

"Tim, start the engine of the gyro! Get it going before it freezes. Check the fuel, old timer—get it ready to hop!"

"Sure, Jimmy!"

Tim hurried out the east entrance as Operator 5 turned back.

Jimmy Christopher found Z-7 now at the telephone, rasping orders over the line to WDC-13, the central Intelligence headquarters.

"Connect with all our operators as rapidly as possible. Instruct them to come to WDC-13 and to take the utmost care to conceal their movements. They are to be held ready for important orders!"

OPERATOR 5 said to the President, as Z-7 straightened: "Sir, there is slim chance that we can defend the Capital if invaders attack it. Our men will be rendered helpless by the terrific cold. Washington will be paralyzed exactly as New York was; every government building will be seized. Regardless of everything else, sir, your personal safety must be considered. I beg of you to leave Washington before the invasion actually begins."

Z-7 blurted: "An invasion while this cold lasts will mean complete disruption of the government!"

"Exactly that," Operator 5 replied grimly. "But it must not mean making the President prisoner of the enemy!"

The Chief Executive, gazing in consternation out the window, along a street which was rapidly becoming deeply banked with hard-packed snow, made a gesture of hopelessness.

"The storm is blocking the roads even now. There are a dozen stalled cars within sight. No trains will be able to run—no planes take off from the fields here. Your warning, Operator 5, is futile. How can I leave the city now?"

Jimmy Christopher heard—above the howling of the storm—a muffled roar from the lawn behind the White House.

It was the irregular beat of an engine which rapidly smoothed off. He answered urgently:

"That's my autogyro, sir—at your disposal. It can fly now because of its short take-off, but soon even that will be impossible. It is dangerous—but there isn't any other way. I urge you to make use of it, sir—immediately!"

Z-7 added quickly: "By all means use the gyro, Mr. President. It's impossible to say how far the storm area extends, but if you act quickly you can escape it. Until it is possible to set up a temporary White House, I suggest the use of Intelligence headquarters BM at Baltimore. It is well-hidden—you will be safe there."

A flash of decision lighted the President's eyes. Operator 5 stepped from the study again; his quick gesture summoned the secretary toward the Chief Executive. The White House detail came to Operator 5's side as he strode to the east entrance. Peering through the beating snow, he saw the gyro faintly, its wings already laden, with Tim Donovan huddling at the throttle. He braced the door shut against the icy blasts and quickly explained the critical situation to the Secret Service squad.

"Since your duty demands it," he declared, "one of you will accompany the President—but one only. To tax the plane in this wind might crash it. In an emergency like this ordinary regulations must be forgotten."

The chief of the White House detail answered promptly: "That's my job, Operator 5."

The door of the study opened; the President strode near, bundling a heavy coat around him. The penetrating sting of the

ATTACK OF THE BLIZZARD MEN

The turret-guns sprayed
death at the Secret Service
men and the auto gyros!

cold was already almost unbearable. Jimmy Christopher gripped the knob to open the way and said:

"I'll fly you to BM, sir."

THE PRESIDENT, turning quickly to the chief of the White House detail, asked: "You hold a pilot's license, don't you, Harkiss?" He received the eager answer, "Yes, sir!" His numb hand went to Operator 5's arm.

"My boy, we need the Intelligence now as never before. It is one of our chief weapons against the invaders. We must preserve it at all costs. Your orders are to remain at Z-7's side."

"Yes, sir."

The President's chilled fingers gripped Operator 5's and Z-7's. He turned to shoulder out into the blinding storm, when Operator 5's touch on his shoulder suddenly stopped him. Harkiss, now in a heavy coat, paused alarmed in the open door. Snow gusted into the corridor as Operator 5 listened with whitening face....

Through the shrieking of the storm the drumming of the gyro carried—but now there was another sound that brought to Jimmy Christopher's heart a chill even sharper than that in the air. It was a deafening, grinding, clanking sound which came from the avenue.

A tank!

Operator 5 shouldered out the door and peered through the blinding swirl of snow. The President, Z-7 and Harkiss crowded behind him, struggling through a drift mounting against the wall. Through the veil of white, they peered at an ominous black movement beyond the gate. They saw it crawling, turn-

ing toward the drive of the
White House—a massive,
steel war-monster with
machine guns bristling in
its superstructure!

"Get to the gyro!"
Operator 5's voice rang
sharply through the howl
of the wind. "Mr. Presi-
dent—to the gyro!"

He plunged through
the drift, gripping the President's arm, while Z-7 struggled
with them. The tearing wind, the drifting snow, were handicaps
which made each step an ordeal. The gyro was dimly visible as
they plunged into the icy blasts—and behind them the roaring
din of the tank mounted. As they fought desperately to reach
the craft in which Tim Donovan was waiting, a crash echoed
through the storm.

Operator 5 saw the massive tank driving against the closed
gate. Under its tremendous power, the posts were torn from their
sockets. A cloud of flying white sprang up as the tank breasted
a deep drift, and its caterpillar treads sent it crawling ponder-
ously over the wrecked gate. It vanished, then reappeared, its
speed quickening; and now it sped with swinging guns toward
the historic mansion.

Operator 5's ringing voice hurried the President and Harkiss toward the gyro. The density of the falling snow obscured
their movements but Jimmy Christopher realized that the snow

offered no obstacle to the tank. A single powerful blast from its guns could hurl instant death across the snow—could, in a moment, make the President of the United States a freezing corpse on the White House grounds. That dread possibility became magnified as the snarling clatter of the approaching tank grew louder.

Jimmy Christopher's command sent Tim Donovan sprawling down over the gyro's cowling. Hastily, the Chief Executive and Harkiss climbed up. The savagery of a polar cyclone beat around the craft as Harkiss released the brakes and thrust the throttle wide. The burst of power sounded an alarm which turned the tank directly toward the spot—an ominous shadow of doom advancing through the swirling snow.

"Take it up!" Operator 5 shouted desperately.

THE SECRET SERVICE men around him had drawn their guns—but the weapons were useless against the steel-cased war monster. The gyro's engine thundered as it shook snow from its vanes, as its fat wheels turned against hard-packed white. Operator 5 forgot the biting cold in his concern for the President during that treacherous take-off. The craft struggled, moved, then bounded. It sprang into the air with its propeller and spinning blades slashing through the gusting flurries—and at the instant it soared, the beat of a machine gun broke through the storm.

"Down!"

Operator 5's warning carried through the first tattoo of the weapon. He flung himself into the deep snow, and felt Tim Donovan and Z-7 fall beside him. The white stuff covered them coldly as they lay with slugs singing a vicious hymn of hate about them. The North Pole coldness might freeze them alive if they were forced to remain motionless too long, and it offered them no protection against the whining bullets. Heart pounding, knowing there was no defense against the tank, Jimmy Christopher heard the snarling of its machinery as it sped to the spot where the gyro had lifted.

The White House Secret Service squad retreated before the monster's advance, their guns cracking out a foolhardy challenge. Bullets *spanged* off the metal plates of the tank as it sped. The guns in its turret spread like death-pointing fingers. Two swung upward toward the shadow-like gyro in the air. Two swiveled toward the dismayed Secret Service men. At the same instant, four muzzles spouted fountains of fire into the churning snow.

Choking, agonized cries mingled with the stuttering chorus of guns. A withering fire raked across the scattering Secret Service men. A storm of lead, more violent than the arctic tempest struck them as they attempted to flee through the thick drifts. They plunged down, and the white around them was stained red. Desperately, Operator 5 twisted up to see them— the loosely sprawled figures of the dead already being blanketed with thick flakes; the tragic struggles of the dying attempting to escape the horror of the freezing doom.

"Keep down!" he warned again, to Tim Donovan and Z-7, as he twisted to peer at the snarling monster of attack.

Its raised guns were pounding bullets into the sky, swinging to follow the erratic movements of the gyro. It was a bobbing shadow in the opaque sky. The gunners in the tank ceased their fire and the huge machine turned, sped across the White House grounds. As it drew away, Operator 5 brought himself alertly to his knees. He crouched, body numbed by the cruel cold, and mumbled through blue lips:

"Get to the White House! Keep low!"

Z-7 and Tim Donovan rose to scurry after him as he darted ahead. As he zigzagged from mound to mound, keeping in cover as much as possible, the boy and the Washington chief followed the trail he made. Together they struggled breathless and chilled to the front of the historic dwelling.

Z-7 thrust in through the east entrance. As he pushed the door shut against the furor of the wind, he glimpsed Operator 5 and Tim Donovan fighting their way along the front of the building. He ignored the frantic questions of the terrorized men and women inside as he sped to the President's study. His voice crackled over the telephone wire as he called WDC-13.

"V-4!" he exclaimed when he obtained connection with the special agent who held command of the central headquarters during his absence. "Phone all important government officials as rapidly as possible!" He noted that the instrument was affected by the cold, and in his desperation he shouted. "Above all, reach the cabinet members, and warn them to get out of the city as fast as possible. I don't know how they'll be able to make it—but they've got to try to escape the city!"

Z-7, TURNING in a frenzy from the desk, glanced through the frosted window to see Operator 5 jerking open a door to the massive sedan sitting in front of the White House. He sped along the corridor, quickly seizing the bundle of coats the President's secretary offered him. When he ducked out into the storm and struggled to the sedan, he saw that Jimmy Christopher had the choke full out, the throttle thrust wide open. Operator 5, as Z-7 slipped into the car, kept the starter grinding in a desperate effort to start the motor in spite of the intense cold.

Jimmy Christopher's heart speeded with dread, for the overtaxed battery was being drained; but he kept the motor turning over. He called back urgently: "Lock the doors! Make sure the windows are tight!" Still using the self-starter, he peered through the frosted glass to see weird figures marching in squad formation past the broken gate.

They were men enveloped in strange garments of metal scales that glittered in the frosty light of the sun. Bearing side-arms and rifles, they followed a commander toward the White House. Through the thick goggles of their metal helmets their eyes gleamed at Operator 5 in the car. And as their officer shouted a curt command, they broke ranks and swarmed toward the sedan.

"Let them come!" Operator 5 exclaimed. "This is the President's armored car.* They won't be able to touch us—"

* AUTHOR'S NOTE: The following is a dispatch of the Associated Press, recently distributed: "Bullet-proofed over every square inch of their surfaces,

"But if that motor doesn't start, we'll be trapped in here!" Z-7 gasped. "We'll be frozen like—"

The motor snorted—then died. Desperately, Operator 5 pressed the starter again—and power surged. He fingered the choke and throttle with the utmost care as the mailed raiders swarmed around the car. The officer, stopping near Operator 5, deliberately aimed an automatic. His command, thickly accented, was: "You are our prisoners! Come out!" Operator 5's numb lips curved into a tight smile as he pulled the gear lever, made sticky by the cold, and released the clutch.

The first spin of the sedan's wheels in the packed snow precipitated a fusillade of bullets from the guns of the mailed invaders. Deafening concussions rocked inside the car as the bullets *spanged* against tough steel and non-shatterable glass. The windows webbed with white cracks as Jimmy Christopher sent the sedan spurting away. It slipped, slewed dangerously as it twisted toward the broken gate. Smashing bullets pursued as the sedan went careening into the avenue. Knowing that the mailed troops were aiming at the car's tires, he plunged it frantically through mountainous drifts.

two Pierce-Arrow limousines have been sent to Washington for the use of the President and the Director of the Bureau of Investigation of the Department of Justice, it was learned tonight.

"The cars are equipped with bullet-proof glass in windshields and windows, and the bodies have been reinforced with heavy steel sheeting to make them safe against almost any kind of bullet. The machines are capable of making 110 miles per hour."

Inside that lurching fort on wheels, Operator 5, Tim Donovan and Z-7 peered through hoary panes at an appalling scene.
As they sped past heaped intersections, they saw squad after
squad of mailed invaders marching toward the center of the
Capital. As they sought shelter, they glimpsed snarling parades
of tanks with turret guns swinging, speeding to strategic points.
With appalling swiftness, with overwhelming confidence, the
forces of the invaders were swarming to positions of control—
while terrifying cold paralyzed the nerve-centers of the nation's
government....

CHAPTER 4
SURROUNDED HEADQUARTERS

TOWARD THE domed Capitol—a mountain of
white in the arctic wilderness of the city—mailed troops
advanced. Out of the radiating avenues, giant tanks came
swarming. A ring of enemy steel formed around the historic
building, taking command, while at a hundred scattered strategic points over the length and breadth of the city, other detachments of armored troops and mobile forts appeared as if by
black magic.

Out of the ice-caked Potomac, a fleet of black submarines
appeared, the chattering machine-guns on their superstructures
manned by weirdly uniformed crews. Rumbling concussions
broke through the silence of the cold as torpedoes rammed boats
in the river. Other tanks went swarming across Boiling Field,
where planes lay buried under deep drifts. From all over the city

echoed the rattling of machine-guns as the merciless drive of the enemy left hundreds of freezing corpses in the snow-banks....

Over the almost impassable roads radiating from the Capital, detachments of United States Infantry struggled. Men fought, desperately, to advance, while officers barked agonized commands. United States tanks drove ahead to clear the way. The bitter cold chilled to the bone those infantrymen who were forced to fight for every step. Some dropped exhausted, claimed by the lethal power of the cold....

The tanks of the enemy clashed with the tanks of the American army. Metal monsters battled, gun spitting fire while mailed troops swarmed to cut off the advance of the infantry. When it ceased to snow, the horrible intensity of the cold became a dread weapon of powerful advantage to the invaders. Against the guns of the quick moving men in metal, United States soldiers stood no chance. They faced inevitable slaughter.

Blinded by the cold, scarcely able to pull the triggers of their rifles, the roaring guns of the raiders poured death into them. Each devastating burst of fire left scores of American infantrymen sprawled in the bloody snow while hoary death crept over them. Even the crews of the United States tanks were paralyzed by the chill which seized upon them. They struggled to blast their way past the invading war machines, but the invisible enemy—the unseasonable cold—struck them down.

One after another, the American tanks came to a vanquished standstill. Their guns fell silent. The steel monsters of the invaders, swarming past them, plunged among the straggling ranks of the few infantrymen left to face the murderous onslaught.

With the detachments of the American army wiped out before them, enemy tanks and mailed troops confidently advanced to assume complete control of every road.

Metal-clothed officers of the invaders opened the motionless army tanks to find the crews dead—claimed by frigid death.

OVERHEAD, THE sharp thunder of airplane motors rolled. Under the command of the Chief of Staff, a few army and navy battle planes had managed to swoop off snow-laden fields. Their pilots huddled at the sticks, shrinking from the polar blasts of their own propellers. Their observers could scarcely move, or see, as they mumbled directions which sent the crates swinging erratically above the Potomac. They were laden with bombs; their objectives were the sleek-backed submarines lurking in ice-caked water; and added to the insidious menace of the cold came the rending concussions of anti-aircraft shells.

The mailed gun-crews on the superstructure, of the submarines felt none of the paralyzing effect of the bitter chill as they swung the snouts of their archie batteries toward the hovering planes. Instruments of the latest design turned the bursting shells directly upon the winged targets in the sky. Onslaught from the ground made a hell in the heavens....

Dismayed observers found their bomb-releasing mechanisms locked by frozen oil. Pilots felt their motors failing as the cold grew sharper. Each plane was a fragile, brittle thing which threatened to crack apart under its own vibration. The terrific power of the anti-aircraft shells, exploding with roars like mocking laughter, swept doom among straggling crates.

Flying shrapnel and churning air tore the army and navy

planes apart. Like fragile glass they shattered before the vicious attack. Fragments of wings and fuselage spilled out of the white sky while the storm of the submarine batteries continued mercilessly. Pilots and observers plunged toward the snow-heaped earth, their muscles numbed, unable to pull the rip-cords of their parachutes. One after another the planes were demolished, until the A.A. batteries went silent, with the last plane down.

Now the awful white silence was broken only by the growling of the invading tanks, and the tramp of mailed troops. The military machine of the raiders continued to function with overwhelming precision. The same master-plan which had gained control of New York now gave the enemy entire domination of Washington....

No vehicle moved except the powerful tanks of the invaders. No figure appeared in the streets save the metal-clad raiders. Their strategic plan gave them a decisive victory just as it had in New York City, adding now complete domination of the machinery of the federal government in Washington....

They circled the great domed Capitol with machines and men of steel. Their movements surrounded the Treasury Buildings. The White House swarmed with mailed troopers. The State, War and Navy Buildings became the headquarters of helmeted commanders. They swooped into every governmental office. Those who were not already victims of the hoary death were felled by the blasting of the invaders' guns. Mercilessly, relentlessly, the power of tile enemy reigned supreme in Washington—except in one suite of hidden rooms.

A detachment of mailed pillagers marched smartly along

a street near the vortex of the city while the commands of an officer sent squads scattering to points of vantage. The officer's goggled eyes turned sharply toward a black sedan parked at the high-banked curb, and his order brought his men to a brisk halt He peered into the car and saw that it was empty. As a lieutenant came smartly to his side, he declared in a foreign tongue:

"This is the special car of the President! There is an excellent reason why it is at this spot. Order a squad to wait and watch it! The others—raid every building in this block!"

IMMEDIATELY, THE mailed troopers swarmed through the frosted doors. They found in every store, every office, every room, men and women who had fallen before the deadly cold. Their goggled eyes searched keenly for the occupants of the President's armored sedan; yet shrewd as they were, they did not discover the secret door in the rear of the grimy restaurant near which die armored car stood.

Managing, for one brief moment, to escape the leaden attack which rained after them as they sped toward this spot, Operator 5, Z-7 and Tim Donovan had darted from the car to the passage hidden behind a closet in the back room of the restaurant Through a secret passage and a concealed elevator they had managed to reach the windowless suite of rooms above.

Hidden within these walls, so cunningly that lifelong residents of Washington might never dream of its existence, was the central headquarters of the United States Intelligence—WDC-13.

They found the rooms frigid, hushed. The automatic heating system was operating, but the sizzling radiators brought scant warmth. The wintry chill had reached into every nook and cranny in the dry, and this headquarters, shrewdly concealed as it was, was not immune.

At their entrance, V-4, acting chief in Z-7's absence, came to them shivering in agony. "Your orders have summoned most of our men here, and they're waiting," he said through stiff lips. "Some of them are missing—I'm afraid the cold has got them. In God's name, what can we do to protect ourselves?"

Z-7 snapped: "We've got to hold this headquarters. If we lose it, our last stand against the enemy in Washington is gone. Any word from BM?"

"Our communications system is almost out of commission," V-4 answered with a shudder. "None of the teletypes is working. There is only one means left—wireless. Even that—"

Operator 5 strode past and thrust into the communications-room. Usually it was a humming hive, with a bank of teletypes clattering, telephone switchboards flashing, radio installations busy. Now the vital nerve center was almost completely paralyzed and the room hushed. The chief-dispatcher rose anxiously as Jimmy Christopher entered.

"There's a message coming in from BM now," he declared through chattering teeth, "so faint we can hardly catch it." As Operator 5 strode to the panel where a wireless expert was clamping cold phones to his ears and writing with a blue hand, the dispatcher followed. "Cold weather usually makes wireless signals crisper, but this installation is hardly functioning at all."

Operator 5 lifted the auxiliary receiver. "Can you raise New York by telephone?" he asked quickly.

"No. The lines are dead."

Z-7 had followed quickly. "Watch the long distance trunks for any report that might come through," he directed, "but ignore any local signals. It's certain the enemy has seized control of the public telephone system. Any incoming call from Washington might betray the location of this headquarters."

"Yes, sir!"

Listening over the auxiliary headset, Jimmy Christopher heard faintly singing signals that were struggling through the vacuous ether. Dots and dashes, scarcely audible, formed words in his mind. He listened intently while the expert's pencil jerked.

"Special Z-7 through BM. The President has arrived safely in Baltimore and is coming now by car to BM. Information received through Herrick. This city is not affected by the cold. Weather unchanged."

Grimly, Z-7 commanded: "Flash BM to stand ready to act as central headquarters in case of emergency. If WDC-13 is discovered by the invaders, we must have an established means of communications with our field forces. Get that message through before the equipment fails."

THE WIRELESS operator began to pound the key with stiff fingers as Z-7, Jimmy Christopher and Tim Donovan left the communications-room. Their faces were grave as V-4 led them toward an office at the end of the corridor. They stepped in to find the room filled with Intelligence agents who had responded to Z-7's urgent orders. Tortured by the cold, they were huddling about the radiators. As Z-7 strode to face them, they shiveringly snapped to attention.

"Gentlemen," his crackling voice came, "Washington is being subjugated by an armed invasion. Have you any reports?"

The dismayed men blurted out their information. Struggling through the storm to WDC-13, they had glimpsed movements of the enemy tanks and troops which, pieced together, supplied the Washington chief with a picture of the operations of the invasion. The reports of his men confirmed his fears that the foe had annihilated the District police, had seized all newspaper plants, banks, broadcasting stations, telephone exchanges, and the telegraph systems. They had assumed control of all power plants and were barricading all roads. Transportation and communication was at a standstill due both to the storm and the merciless strategy of the invaders.

"First the financial center of the nation, now the seat of the federal government—the people of both cities completely at the mercy of the invaders!" Z-7 exclaimed bitterly. "We alone have escaped the trap. There is a master plan operating, gentlemen, which will destroy us at the first opportunity. Such a crisis as this demands that you forget families, homes, and friends. You men, here in this room—you are our only hope of combating the invaders."

An oppressive sense of the enemy's power came to Operator 5 as he listened. Beyond these secret walls, the invaders reigned supreme. Surrounded by a merciless military machine, WDC-13 had become a secret fortress of the Intelligence, which alone had escaped their penetration.

"This," Z-7 continued raspingly, "is the most urgent challenge we have ever met. For long months, the commanders of the invaders have undoubtedly been planning this move. We are pitted against the shrewdest, most ruthless military organization in the world, and have been caught by surprise. But in spite of every disadvantage, in spite of every handicap, we must maintain our organization—for now there is no other in Washington capable of combating the enemy."

Operator 5 searched the pinched faces of the men in the room. He noted deep lines of agony on the face of an agent standing near the corridor door. S-12, one of the youngest men in the service, gazed at Z-7 with eyes that betrayed unbearable torment raging within him. While every other man was intent on Z-7's words, S-12 quietly opened the door—and Jimmy Christopher's nerves tightened warily.

"We can only guess the vast ramifications of this plan of invasion," Z-7 declared sharply. "But we can be sure that every move of the enemy was carefully laid out by a military genius months ago. Tanks turned against us—brought into the country, certainly, piece by piece, labeled probably as industrial machinery, and secretly assembled at scores of hidden points. Tanks—a weapon even more to be feared than bombers and combat planes!"

Operator 5 moved quietly toward the door as S-12 slipped out of the room....

"**TRAINED TROOPS** raised among the aliens within our shoes, enemies who have entered the country both legally and illegally. Among them men who have conformed to the ritual of becoming American citizens while their true allegiance lies with the foreign powers of which they are still considered subjects.

Special uniforms, also brought past our customs under false declarations. Ammunition smuggled across our borders. In our very midst, this mighty machine of war has been constructed. It has struck two terrific, crippling blows and, here in Washington, we are the only protective agency of the government still functioning—our armor, gentlemen, is absolute secrecy."

Quietly Jimmy Christopher closed the door. As he strode along the corridor, Tim Donovan hurried at his side. The door of the communications-room opened as they neared it; the chief-dispatcher and the wireless expert strode out together.

"Operator 5, the radio has completely failed! The telephone alone is the only means of communication we have left—and that is failing. Z-7 must know—"

Jimmy Christopher's eyes darkened as the two men strode on. He listened through the door of the dispatch-room and heard a voice speaking in a whisper. Quietly he twisted the knob, and peered through a crack. The sight he saw filled him with dismay—S-12, seated at the switchboard, speaking anxiously into the transmitter.

Operator 5 caught a few terse words as he strode toward S-12. "Mary! You've got to get out of the city if you can! If you stay—!" Jimmy Christopher's hand flashed to the cam and broke the connection. He tore the receiver from S-12's hand as S-12 jerked to his feet.

"You can't do that! Let me talk to her! Good God, if she stays—!"

Jimmy Christopher's voice crackled. "S-12, you've violated the Chief's orders—endangered this headquarters and every man

64

in the Washington unit. You dared call a public phone from this number—knowing the invaders are in control of the exchange! If that message is traced, we're lost!"

S-12's face went white. "I—I couldn't think of anything else but warning her. She's the girl I love—we're going to be married. You can't expect me to do nothing to help her when these damned devils are swarming—!"

"You're expected to serve the Intelligence first!" Jimmy Christopher interrupted firmly. "Your highest allegiance is to the Service. Get away from this switchboard and stay away. I sympathize with you. I understand. But you've risked the life of every man in the Washington division, and for that you deserve court-martial!"

S-12 mumbled: "God, I—I'm sorry. I couldn't think of anything, but—" He straightened, his eyes shining with worry. "Do you think they'll be able to trace the message? How can they find us when—?"

"The invaders know there's an Intelligence headquarters in this city," Jimmy Christopher answered tightly. "It's equally certain they've been searching for it. There are enemy officers at the switchboard through which your call passed. If they have a mobile wireless unit nearby—flash the alarm to them—" His dark eyes flashed. "I do not intend to inform on you, S-12—but your duty is to report your own actions to the Chief."

S-12 muttered: "Yes—yes, I understand that."

HE WALKED uncertainly along the corridor toward the room where Z-7 was still speaking to his band of undercover operators. He entered slowly, his face picturing profound dismay.

Operator 5 and Tim Donovan watched him as he stood aside, gazing at the hard, grim face of Z-7.

"Gee, Jimmy," the boy whispered. "He'll get broken for it, won't he?"

"Perhaps, Tim," Operator 5 answered quietly. "I'm sorry as the devil for him—but in this crisis the Service must stand above everything else. Di and Dad are in New York, in the very center of the invaders there, but even if we could reach them somehow, we wouldn't dare."

Z-7's voice was crackling imperative orders. "Cover yourselves in every way possible. Make your reports to the men at the substations I have designated, and make them in person. Trust nothing to writing, do not risk using the wires. Substation chiefs must report directly here, taking every means of covering your movements. If we are discovered—if WDC-13 by any chance falls into the hands of the enemy—we are lost!"

A chill more penetrating than the bite of the air coursed along Operator 5's nerves. He was the first to hear the hollow, crashing sound which reverberated along the corridor. It came from some point below—from, Jimmy Christopher realized, the base of the hidden elevator which gave access to WDC-13! The rhythmic crashing could only mean that smashing axes were opening the way—that the invaders were breaking in!

Operator 5 spun as startled exclamations broke from the men in the room. Z-7 strode toward the door, his face white as death, dismay smoldering in his dark eyes. S-12 followed him with slow steps; his eyes reflected agony. Muffled voices carried along the corridor, reaching every man in that hushed room.

"Batter it down!"

Jimmy Christopher sped into Z-7s office and swung open the leaf of a recess in the hall. His hand closed hard on the handle of a knife-switch as he pulled it open. It controlled the motor which actuated the secret elevator; behind his move was a hope that it would balk the raiders. But even as he turned away, louder crashes sounded beyond—the cleaving of axes through wood.

Operator 5 jerked open the door to see the gleaming blades splintering through the elevator panel. Swift as his move had been to break the circuit, it had not stopped the raiders below the level of the secret offices. Their powerful blows were shattering the sliding door as Jimmy Christopher sped back along the corridor. He stopped short, listening to the breathless voice of S-12 speaking to the appalled Z-7.

"I'm responsible, sir! I disobeyed orders—made a telephone call to my fiancée to warn her! It led them here! I—I'm sorry, chief!"

" 'Sorry!' " Z-7 grated. "You may well be sorry, S-12. This means that our Washington Intelligence unit is utterly destroyed! You're under arrest!"

Operator 5 exclaimed: "The emergency exit, Chief—we've got to use it!"

Z-7 whirled to snap: "Every man out the emergency exit!"

JIMMY CHRISTOPHER, Tim Donovan and the Washington chief hurried farther back along the corridor as the resounding blows of the axes echoed like the knocking of the hand of doom. A section had been driven out of the elevator panel; hands in mailed gloves were groping through. The secret agents crowded into a small room at the rear of the suite as Operator 5 stayed at the door and watched in dismay.

He heard a faint grinding of machinery, and knew that Z-7 was at the controls of another secret elevator which never before had been used. It had been provided for use in extreme emergency; and that was now at hand. A glance backward showed Operator 5 that the Intelligence men were crowding into the cab. When it could bold no more, the panel slipped shut and the cage began to descend. Tim Donovan and S-12 remained in the room.

Operator 5 glimpsed a mailed figure shouldering through the broken panel of the forward elevator. A huge man—a gleaming apparition in fish-scaled metal—charged along the corridor. His eyes gleamed triumphantly through the goggles of his metal helmet as Jimmy Christopher's hand flashed gun-ward. Instantly the weapon of the mailed invader blasted a challenge. Jimmy Christopher's automatic met it with a rocking fusillade.

He staggered back against the door as the tearing power of a bullet struck his left arm. The impact brought stunning agony to his cold-tortured body. He knew that his slugs had flown true— but that the mailed suit of the invader had deflected them. He saw other metal-clad figures bursting into the corridor as the first rushed toward him.

He attempted to thrust the door shut; but the enemy's shoulder blocked it. Tim Donovan, striving desperately to close the door at Operator 5's side, caught at the mailed hand as it aimed a gun directly at Jimmy Christopher. The blast of the weapon rocked deafeningly in the room. As the slug bored into the floor. Operator 5 deliberately opened the way.

The metal-garbed figure stumbled in and whirled with leveled weapon. Tim Donovan slapped the door shut and shot a bolt into its socket a moment before heavy fists hammered on it. In the room, the single member of the invading forces straightened with eyes gleaming through his goggles. He faced Operator 5 while the dismayed Tim Donovan and the wretched S-12 watched.

The automatics of Jimmy Christopher and S-12 were leveled at the raider; and, through the thick lenses of the goggles, they saw his triumphant eyes wrinkle in a confident smile.

"I had hoped," a guttural voice came through the mesh of the metal helmet, "to come face to face with you, Operator 5."

Desperately S-12 fired. The crash of his gun blended with the heavy hammering on the door as other raiders attempted to break their way in. Under the impact of the bullet, the metal-clad figure winced—but nothing more. He straddled, his huge gun leveled, his eyes still wrinkling with an evil smile of victory.

"I had hoped," the accented tones came again, "for the privilege of killing you, Operator 5."

Tim Donovan's widened eyes saw the mailed finger tighten on the trigger of the massive automatic; and he leaped frantically. His hand struck the weapon the instant it exploded, as Jimmy Christopher leaped aside. The bullet *spanged* against the steel wall of the room. A wrathful roar broke from the lips of the enemy officer as Operator 5 hurled himself across the room.

Tim Donovan continued to grip the huge fist that held the

gun as Operator 5 struck a powerful blow into the hooded face of the officer who staggered back. Jimmy Christopher dropped his gun. His hands flashed to the lower edge of the mesh cowl, and he ripped it loose. The other mailed hand struck a dazing blow at the side of his head, but he clung, pressing his thumbs with swift certainty against vital nerve-centers in the enemy's neck.

AN EXPLOSION of hot breath sounded inside the hood; a paralytic stiffness seized the man in mail. Operator 5 stepped back alertly as the metal-clad figure stiffened and toppled. The officer plunged to the floor while sledgehammer blows crashed on the outside of the metal door, loosening it in its frame. As Jimmy Christopher grimly reached down to the hood of the fallen officer, he heard the elevator machinery grinding and knew that the cab was rising. He was in the act of removing the mask when a movement behind him drew his startled eyes.

He saw S-12 slumped in despair against the wall, a revolver turned into his mouth, the hammer of the weapon drawing back.

Operator 5's move was lightning swift. His hand flashed to S-12's wrist and jerked it up. At that instant the gun exploded. The ballet screamed off the metal wall as S-12 staggered back, blinded by the flame. Operator 5 tore the gun away and pocketed it.

"I'm to blame for this!" the young agent blurted in agony. "It's my fault—mine! I can't bear to face—"

"Your life," Operator 5 interrupted savagely, "still belongs to the service!"

As he thrust S-12 toward the panel of the elevator, a flash of hissing flame drew his startled eyes toward the embattled door. A tongue of blinding white fire was licking through a rapidly widening orifice. It sliced swiftly through the steel of the door as Operator 5 backed toward the elevator panel, automatic leveled.

"Jimmy!" Tim Donovan blurted. "It's an acetylene torch. We can't keep them out now!"

The sibilance of the flame mingled with the grinding of the rising elevator as Operator 5 took swift aim. Three times he blasted bullets through the widening hole in the steel door. The flame did not stop eating its way; the mailed suits of the invaders were proof against Operator 5's bullets. He knew that the raiders must surely reach the hidden elevator—that nothing could keep them out of it As Jimmy Christopher seized the rigid officer, the elevator panel slid open behind him.

Z-7, muttering his amazement, sprang out of the cab and rapidly assisted Jimmy Christopher in lifting the unconscious officer into the cab. Tim Donovan and S-12 followed as a clanging crash echoed in the room. A ragged section of the door dropped away as Z-7 thrust the elevator panel shut Operator 5 fired desperately through the narrow opening as armored men charged into the room with spitting guns. The panel clicked shut; the cage glided downward; and again a sharp, hissing sound warned that the relentless raiders were intent on opening the way.

"We can't stop them, chief!" Jimmy Christopher exclaimed in dismay.

Z-7 answered grimly: "Our only hope is to slip out and scat-

KARLE KRAN

KADA
ALDEE

COMMISSAR
EVOL KRAN

S-12
ENDO
ORVELLO

ter. If the Washington unit is able to function at all now, it will be under the greatest handicaps—without headquarters!"

The whispering of the greedy acetylene torch was still audible when the cab stopped. Quickly Operator 5 carried the hooded captive along a brick passageway, while Z-7, S-12 and Tim Donovan followed.

The underground corridor along which they hurried was part of a far-reaching web of interlinking tunnels. Through it scattered parts of the city could be reached through cunningly concealed exits. Constructed as a precaution against invasion, it now served its purpose. In a large room off one side, the secret agents had gathered, shuddering with the cold. Their breath steamed as Z-7 snapped orders:

"Each operator must act on his own. Your posts have been designated. Your work begins now—and it cannot end, for any one of you, except with death. Find your way out!"

THE WRETCHED S-12 kept at Z-7s side as the chief left the underground room. In a small cubicle in another branch of the tunnel, he found Operator 5 and Tim Donovan bending over the mailed captive. The room was dark; Z-7 paused to peer in amazement. For in the gloom the uniform of the enemy officer was shining with a phosphorescent light.

Grimly Operator 5 pulled the metal mask from the unconscious prisoner's face. Amazement filled him as he gazed at the strong, square chin, the powerful mouth, the beetling brow. He rose and said quietly to Z-7: "In the code message I intercepted, the name of Commissar Evol Kran was mentioned. This man is Karle Kran, the Commissar's son!"

74

Z-7 declared vehemently: "He remains our prisoner. We've got to get out of these tunnels at once, Operator 5. If the invaders discover the exits and close us in—"

The thought hurried the chief back along the corridor. Tim Donovan hastened to aid him in swinging a ponderous door into its heavy frame. It was a cement slab reinforced with iron which could resist the torch and the hammers of the enemy. Once it thudded shut, Z-7 slid a stout bar into deep sockets. He returned to the cell with the breathless Tim Donovan to find Operator 5 stripping the uniform from Karle Kran.

"We've got to leave him here, Chief," Jimmy Christopher declared. "He may become valuable to us—and this uniform may reveal the secret of the cold."

He closed a door of stout iron bars as he spoke, turned a heavy key, and gave it to Z-7. With the metal-scaled garment bundled under Operator 5's arm, they hurried along the winding passage. Under the orders of Z-7, the other men of the service had already sought their way out the hidden exits. Their footfalls were muffled echoes as they hurried toward the secret doors....

Men in mail had stationed themselves in the offices of WDC-13. In the communications-room, the center of a network of special wires stretching to sub-headquarters scattered all over the United States, officers issued sharp commands which placed all the vital, complex organism of the American Intelligence under their control. Their blow paralyzed the nervous system of the entire service.

A mail-clad lieutenant advanced, snapped a salute to the

captain in charge. "The Americans have escaped, sir. We have no captives—and Major Kran is missing!"

"So?" came drawlingly through the hood of the commander. "No word must reach Commissar Kran. We must do everything possible to find the Major. If the Commissar learns of this, he will blame us for it and order every one of us shot!"

"But we cannot pass the heavy door in the passage below, Captain! We know no other way of getting into the space beyond. The Major is a prisoner there—"

"Find him!" The order was a bellow. "Stop at nothing to find him!"

METAL HEELS clicked as the lieutenant withdrew. A buzzing sound in a booth at the side of the communications-room caught the attention of the captain. Turning quickly, he saw that one of the teletype instruments was beginning to function stiffly. Each letter a slow snap, a message began to form on the curling, yellow tape. As the captain watched, a second lieutenant advanced and saluted: "The cold is alleviating, sir."

"Yes, yes! That is why this machine is starting to work again. The force is being decreased."

"It means our conquest of Washington is complete, sir! We have established ourselves absolutely in the American capital!"

"And the next step in our march toward victory over the entire United States, Lieutenant," the captain answered with a slow smile, "is that now being taken."

He indicated the words forming on the yellow teletype tape—words pronouncing a sentence of doom on a third great key city of the nation:

... WDC-13... TERRIFIC COLD DESCENDING ON CHICAGO....

CHAPTER 5
SPY'S COMMISSION

A S STRANGELY and as swiftly as it had come, the cold moderated over Washington. Compared with the deadly, bitter frigidity which had paralyzed the city, the temperature became bearable; life in the open became possible again. But the mercury still stood low in the thermometer columns; streets remained heaped with banks of snow; the uncanny winter still held sway; and in the hearts of those it had trapped, a dread remained that the awful white silence would return once more.

The population of Washington had been decimated by the toll of the cold. Residents who had survived the calamity ventured into the streets to find them patrolled by metal-garbed troops; tanks were stationed around government buildings and strategic points. They discovered themselves prisoners within the encircled city, slaves of a merciless military machine.

In their struggle to procure food and shelter, they found every market manned by the invaders; every source of coal, oil and wood under the control of mailed men. Their wildest protests were silenced by drawn guns; their active resistance was quelled by blasting bullets. There was no law in Washington now save that of the invaders. Disobedience meant a death sentence, without trial, without any possible appeal.

When newspapers reappeared on the streets, they carried no

dispatches. Then, pages were blackened by ominous instructions laid down by military leaders of the enemy forces. They proclaimed that military law was in effect and announced that a system of food ration cards would be organized at once. They declared that all moneys and securities in the banks had automatically become the property of the war machine. Under no circumstances was any communication allowed with outside points. There was only one concession—permission was granted the residents of the Capitol to leave the city, with the restriction that, once past the armed frontier, return was impossible....

A constant parade of vehicles began to stream past the barricaded roads. No trains moved; no airplanes flew; any boat leaving its pier was certain to be sunk by gunfire or torpedo; the highways alone gave egress from the seized territory. Because thousands of automobiles had been disabled by the freezing cold, each car that passed the barriers was greatly overloaded. Almost penniless, hungry, still suffering from the unseasonal weather, multitudes abandoned their homes and businesses in order to escape the oppression of the military rulers.

A ceaseless stream of cars crawled over the white roads, toward the armed frontiers—a cavalcade of terror. Each was stopped when it reached the border of the invaded territory. There, the occupants were mercilessly stripped of all belongings save only the clothing they wore. Every trunk, case and package was confiscated; every pocket emptied of money, every weapon taken as contraband and every article of jewelry torn away. At each sentry post, the mounds of seized articles grew higher; and the cars crawled on....

A COUPÉ which once had been devoted to the service of the Intelligence slowed when it was safely past the border. The young man at the wheel turned up the rubber floor-mat, retrieved three bright objects which had been concealed there. One was a silver case containing credentials, signed by the President of the United States, identifying him as Operator 5.

The second was a slender, gold chain, on which dangled an ornament Jimmy Christopher prized above everything—a tiny, golden skull-and-crossbones with eyes of rubies.

He passed the third object, a ring, to Tim Donovan. It was emblazoned with a death's-head against a background of black, with the mystic numeral 5 on its forehead. It was precious to the boy, for Jimmy Christopher had especially designed it for him, and it was his identification as Operator 5's unofficial assistant. They were grimly silent as they left embattled Washington behind them and noted the amazing change in the atmosphere.

The wintry whiteness disappeared from the landscape. Snow gave way to fresh green. Though every tree and plant was blighted in the capital, here they were laden with foliage and blossoms. Beyond the armed borders, the devastating effects of the arctic storm had not spread. Within a few moments, the car had passed from a ravaged winterland into a region where summer reigned.

Z-7 peered at Operator 5, completely bewildered. "What the devil is this new weapon they've turned against us?" he asked. "How can we possibly combat that damnable cold if it strikes again?"

Jimmy Christopher's eyes darkened with thought; his answer

came quietly: "I can only guess, Chief, but the cold power must certainly be one which only now is yielding to the investigations of science. It must be electrical in character—a frequency of vibration far down in the spectrum, in the band not yet completely understood. I believe that, whatever this deadly influence is, it does not project cold, but cold is simply its result."

As the car gathered speed over the open highway, Z-7 mused puzzled: "I don't understand what you mean, Operator 5."

"If I'm right Chief, the scientific facts behind the cold-projector are quite simple. Everything, living as well as inanimate bodies, is composed of molecules, built up from atoms. The atomic structure of all matter is constantly in vibration. Heat increases the speed of these moving particles—which are in reality electrical charges—and the extent to which they travel. Cold has the opposite effect. That is the reason, for instance, while most metals and all gases expand when they are heated and contract when they are chilled."

"I understand," the Chief said.

"Exactly. The lower the temperature, the less the activity of atomic particles. There is a temperature at which, theoretically, all atomic activity will cease. This point is called absolute zero. It is a temperature far below the zero of the Fahrenheit or Centigrade scales. It is the temperature of empty, cosmic space—it is believed!—The lowest possible. It is actually a fraction lower than 273 degrees below zero, Centigrade.

"Scientists have almost attained absolute zero in their experiments on the atomic structure of matter. They have done this by evaporating liquid helium—the most difficult of all gases to liquefy. At that temperature, the electrical activity of atoms theoretically comes to a standstill; matter becomes absolutely dead in the fullest meaning of the word."

Z-7 AND Tim Donovan listened intently as Jimmy Christopher turned the car into the outskirts of Baltimore.

"The action of the new war machine," Operator 5 continued, "must in some way electrically impede the atomic activity of whatever lies within its field. The effect of the projector, in other words, must be to absorb the electrical charges within the atom. This blotting-up of energy slows down the atomic motions. As the slackening process advances and a state of molecular rest is approached, coldness results. The slower the internal activity, the more intense the cold—and this damnable device of the enemy evidently is capable of controlling the cold effect"

"Whatever this force is," Z-7 declared grimly, "we must find a way to combat it or the invaders will be able to subdue the entire nation!"

"I am afraid, Chief," Operator 5 answered, "that the most obvious means of protection will fail. But because we are almost completely ignorant about the force, we've got to try them out."

Jimmy Christopher drew the car to a stop near the central business district of Baltimore. With Z-7 and Tim Donovan, he entered an office building, and though an elevator cab was already waiting, they chose to wait for another. It lifted them quickly when Z-7 ordered: "Top floor." When the cab stopped and the grille slid open, the Washington chief added cryptically: "Free State."

"Constitutional," the attendant answered.

"Article Ten."

Immediately the attendant shut the grille again; the cab climbed once more. When the way was next opened, Z-7 led the way into the corridor of a superstructure specially built on the roof of the building. The man in the elevator was an Intelligence operator; these rooms were sub-headquarters BM. Z-7 led Operator 5 and Tim Donovan directly to a door; he knocked a signal, immediately entered. The man who sprang from the desk as the Washington chief entered was N-6, director of the Baltimore area of the Service. He grasped Z-7's hand, but in his agitation, he forgot the formality of a greeting. He uttered a sharp, mirthless laugh as Z-7 quickly inquired: "Have you established direct communication with all other sub-headquarters, N-6? Have you reports?"

"Reports?" the Baltimore director blurted. "I have nothing but reports—the most appalling that have ever come into this office. Read those!"

Z-7s face grew white as he peered at the teletype messages in quick succession. The first stated:

... BM—SPECIAL... PARALYZING COLD WAVE CLOSING DOWN ON PANAMA CANAL ZONE... AIR RECONNAISSANCE IMPOSSIBLE BUT REPORTS OVER FAILING WIRES WARN OF ARMED TROOPS MOVING TOWARD CANAL... POWERFUL FOREIGN TANKS APPROACHING... DEFENSES UNABLE TO REPULSE ATTACK DUE TO STORM AND COLD... PCZ....

Z-7 BLURTED in dismay as his eyes turned to the second report: "They can't resist the invasion! The most vital, the most vulnerable defense unit of the United States—we're certain to lose it!" The second amazing report read:

> … BM… SPECIAL… TERRIFIC STORM STRIK-ING NEW ORLEANS… SUBMARINES FROM GULF CLOSING IN TO BLOCK MISSISSIPPI… DEFENSES POWERLESS BECAUSE OF INTENSE COLD… NOL….

Z-7's sharp glance at the remaining reports picked out the names of vital key cities scattered over the nation: San Francisco, Boston, Seattle, St Louis. Reports had flashed from each, revealing that the devastating cold was striking—that the terrifying storms were spreading destruction and death. The staggering information confirmed Operator 5's conviction that a gigantic and daring master-strategy was in operation.

Z-7 slapped the flimsies to the desk. "Have you been able to reach Washington and New York?" he demanded.

"None of the agents in Washington have been able to get word to us," N-6 answered. "The lines to New York are functioning feebly. The first intelligible message to leak through since the coming of the cold is this—"

Operator 5 leaned forward eagerly to read the terse lines that revealed anew the crushing power of the invading forces:

> … BM… NEW YORK COMPLETELY UNDER CONTROL OF INVADERS… POLICE WIPED OUT AND ARMY POSTS IN RAIDED AREA SCENES

OF TERRIBLE MASSACRE… ALL COMMUNICA-
TION EXCEPT THIS LINE, ALL TRANSPORTATION,
BANKS, NEWSPAPERS, FOOD SUPPLIES, POWER
PLANTS DOMINATED BY MILITARY MACHINE…
UNCONFIRMED REPORTS THAT INVADING
FORCES HAVE ESTABLISHED HEADQUARTERS
IN VERTEX BUILDING… MILLIONS STARVING…
MANHATTAN AN ISLAND OF FROZEN DEAD…
RIVERS AND BAY CLOSELY GUARDED BY SUBMA-
RINES AND NO NAVIGATION ALLOWED… POSSI-
BLE POINTS OF COUNTER-ATTACK: HOLLAND
TUBE RAILROAD TUNNELS AND GEORGE WASH-
INGTON BRIDGE… THIS HEADQUARTERS STILL
HIDDEN BUT INVADERS' ESPIONAGE SYSTEM
CONCENTRATING ON FINDING IT… TS-NY….

"Warn W-8 that the enemy may be listening in through
WDC-13!" Z-7 exclaimed. "He must guard against betraying
his location through these messages. The President is here?"
THE BALTIMORE director promptly led the Washington
chief to a connecting door. Before he passed through, Operator 5 asked quietly: "Is S-12 also here?" Z-7 had ordered S-12
ahead in a separate car, reminding him that he was under arrest
and still a prisoner.

"He's waiting," N-6 replied. "He begged me for orders, but
under the circumstances, I had to refuse."

"If Z-7 has no objection," Operator 5 suggested, "I should
like to have S-12 present now."

The chief hesitated, but nodded permission as he strode

ahead. A second door was opened by the anxious Harkiss, chief of the White House Secret Service detail. A grave-faced man rose from a desk at which he had been reading copies of the appalling reports flashed to BM from the scattered points of attack. The President shook hands heartily with Z-7 and Operator 5.

"I would be a prisoner of the enemy now, at best, except for your warning, Operator 5," he declared earnestly.

"Thanks rather to Harkiss' piloting, Mr. President," Jimmy Christopher answered. "The message that you were safe was the last to reach Washington before we had to abandon WDC-13."

S-12 entered quietly as Operator 5 spoke, and as he heard the words, he winced. Z-7's eyes blazed at him angrily, and he withstood the stare, obviously considering it a just punishment. He stood by, wordless, while the Chief Executive continued:

"In addition to myself, all my cabinet and many members of Congress managed to escape the danger zone. The General Staff withdrew to Fort Meade after the disastrous attempt to retake the Capital. Though we have been forced to abandon Washington, the personnel of the government is largely intact. Major-General Fane's next move is an attempt to drive the enemy from New York.

"The zero hour is tentatively set at dawn tomorrow morning. The maneuvers will demand the careful cooperation of our Infantry, Air Corps and Scout Squadron. Men and planes and ships are moving toward their objective now—and at dawn we strike!"

Operator 5 asked respectfully: "May I make a suggestion,

sir? I hope that the strategy will be made more definite as soon as possible. If the cold closes down again, wireless communication between our defense units may become impossible, and the whole move may be ruined."

The President looked amazed. "But the cold in New York has moderated. Do you believe it will return?"

"When our counter-attack is launched—yes, sir. It is virtually certain. We face a terrific handicap because the enemy is firmly based in New York. They will use the cold-force as a barrier which cannot possibly be crossed if we are unprepared."

"We have undertaken," the President answered, "to provide our men with unusual means of protection. Since the attack on Washington, General Falk ordered special uniforms provided. These are being made now as rapidly as possible and issued to all our units—uniforms provided with a lining of heating coils, supplied by storage batteries carried on the back. The warmth generated in this way will surely protect our men sufficiently?"

OPERATOR 5'S eyes narrowed. "I'm afraid, sir—if the cold-force is what I think it is—" His voice faded. "In any event, the attempt is an excellent one, and an utter necessity. At the same time, sir, I suggest that we try to penetrate into the enemy stronghold. If our armed counter-attack fails, there can be only one method of striking a deadly blow at the invaders and that is through the vulnerable human element in command."

"Commissar Kran is scarcely human!" Z-7 remarked bitterly. "He is the emotionless brains of a ruthless military machine."

"There is a weak point in every man's armor," Jimmy Christopher observed, "and my purpose is to find it in Commissar

86

Kran's. He is in New York, at the military headquarters now established in the Vertex Building, we may be sure." Operator 5 straightened. "Much as I hope the counter-offensive at dawn tomorrow will succeed, I'm afraid there are no usual military tactics which can overcome Kran's war machine and his present tremendous advantage."

The President's anxious eyes searched Jimmy Christopher's face. "Do you mean that our armed defenses are useless?"

Operator 5 pointed out that the United States had been struck by a method of military attack new to the world—the seizure of scattered key points. Already seven of the principal cities of the country, besides the Panamá Canal, were subjugated. In each of these, it was certain, the enemy had planted one of the cold-projectors, a scientific weapon more terrible and more devastating than any other in existence.

"At each point," Jimmy Christopher continued swiftly, "the cold force can and will be used to annihilate our counterattack. As long as that force operates, we face inevitable defeat. Our only hope of driving the invaders out, from a military standpoint, is first to destroy the frigidity projectors. I am afraid it is a tactical problem which cannot be solved by the use of arms alone."

At the very outset, Operator 5 declared, the presence of American non-combatants in the seized key cities was a staggering handicap to the Army and Navy. The presence of the civilian population made it impossible to use cannon and bombs and lethal gas as might be done in an attack on an enemy city. Even more important, the scattered points of invasion made the splitting of our defenses unavoidable. One military victory could not decide the issue of war; to vanquish the enemy, the United States forces must achieve victories at each strategic point.

"And even while we're attempting this," Jimmy Christopher pointed out, "the enemy will be attacking anew at other points. While we're concentrating on counter-attacking certain important cities, the invaders will swarm into others. Our defenses simply cannot cope with that situation, sir. It's hopeless."

The President's face had blanched. "What you say is true— but at the same time, we must make the attempt in spite of certain defeat."

"Yes—but our greatest hope," Operator 5 pressed on, "is to try to crush Commissar Kran personally, as a man and as a commander. For that purpose we must rely upon what remains of our Intelligence system."

Z-7 exclaimed; "I agree with Operator 5's analysis of the situation, Mr. President. The attempt to reach Kran must be made."

"I'd like to undertake that job, Chief," Jimmy Christopher said quietly. "With your permission, I should like to try to penetrate into New York City."

The President said solemnly:

"If you succeed in crossing the enemy's frontier, you will be a spy in enemy territory. Discovery—there is only one penalty—"

"I'm more than willing to risk it," Jimmy Christopher answered.

"Intelligence operators in every one of the invaded cities are facing the same danger. None of us can be considered important or indispensable in this emergency. If I have your approval, Mr. President—Chief—"

"My approval," the President answered, "and my earnest hope that you will succeed, Operator 5. Will you cross that frontier alone?"

"I want Tim Donovan with me, sir, if he is willing to run the risk. Since he's not a member of the Intelligence, no orders can force him to—"

"I'm going with you, Jimmy!" the eager lad exclaimed with a broad smile. "Just try to make me stay back! Sure, I'm going with you!"

"And I—I beg of you to allow me to make the attempt with Operator 5!" S-12 uttered the words huskily as he stepped forward. Z-7's smoldering black eyes turned to his wan, deep-lined face. Operator 5's lips curved in a smile of satisfaction as the Washington chief declared:

"You forget, S-12, that you're under arrest and my prisoner. You must face court-martial for—"

"I'm willing to take my medicine, Chief," S-12 interrupted earnestly. "A court-martial would be altogether justified in ordering me shot. But—I implore you to give me a chance to redeem myself. I'll do my utmost to make up for the foolhardy thing I did, if—"

"Chief," Operator 5 broke in quietly, "I had hoped that S-12 would offer to go with me. That is why I wanted him to be present. He is the one man I want to make the attempt with Tim and me."

Z-7 looked amazed. "The most important detail you have ever undertaken, Operator 5—with scores of completely reliable men who might go with you—and you choose S-12?"

The Holland Tunnels became
an embattled frontier!

"I do, Chief." Jimmy Christopher was studying S-12's pleading eyes. "You must understand, S-12, that the mission may mean death. You will face greater danger than ever before—a situation in which your life or mine may have to be sacrificed to the Service. You must understand that our purpose is all-important, that we must succeed at whatever cost. Knowing that do you still offer to go with me?"

"I do!" S-12 blurted. "I'll pay any price for a chance to vindicate myself. Chief, I beg you to allow me to go with Operator 5."

"If you'll place S-12 in my custody, Chief," Jimmy Christopher suggested, "I will assume full responsibility for him. I realize this is an unprecedented request—but it is also an unprecedented situation we face."

Z-7 answered slowly: "Very well, Operator 5. S-12 is under your orders."

S-12 murmured with pitiable gratitude: "Thanks, Chief! I—I'll do my best!"

The ringing of the telephone turned the President toward it. As he answered the call, his lips tightened and his eyes flashed with alertness. When he lowered the instrument he said crisply:

"The General Staff's tentative plan of counter-attack is now completely prepared. Men and ships and planes are continuing to advance on New York. The zero hour is dawn. Operator 5, when will you make the attempt to cross the enemy's frontier?"

"At dawn, sir," Jimmy Christopher answered promptly, "when our defenses strike."

CHAPTER 6
SIEGE OF MANHATTAN

THE THICK darkness that presages the rising sun was a black shroud over New York—a cold gloom that pervaded every cranny of the invaded metropolis. No window gleamed save those on the topmost floors of the Vertex Building, the highest in the world, where the commanders of the raiders had established their headquarters. The streets were black except for the glare of the electric torches carried by the constantly patrolling men in mail. The oppressive silence was broken only by the tramping of boots and the snarling of crawling tanks. The military genius of Commissar Kran had made Manhattan a stronghold of the enemy.

Within the island, the domination of the mailed troops was an absolute power. All railroad schedules were suspended; no bus depot was operating; every road was barricaded. No river traffic moved; but in the encircling, black water the submarines of the enemy patrolled the island with the mailed gun crews constantly vigilant on their superstructures. On the bridges spanning the streams, squads of the metal-clad men and formations of monster tanks held powerful positions.

The first streak of the rising sun brought the initial move in a historic battle.

Along the roads which fanned from the great George Washington Memorial Bridge on the New Jersey side, massed United States infantry advanced swiftly. They advanced from the darkness as if by magic, executing the first desperate move in the counter-attack mapped by General Staff. With field guns and tanks backing their march, they swarmed upon the western terminus of the gigantic span—an army as grotesque in appearance as the mail-clothed invaders who instantly marshaled to meet them.

Each man was clad in a heavy coat; each wore a leather harness strapped around his shoulders; on the back of every one a storage battery was affixed. With desperate haste, under the orders of General Falk, the infantry had been provided with these garments lined with heating coils. They were not operating when the advance began, for the cold was moderate; but the touch of a switch could bring warmth to the coils. The weight of the batteries and the thickness of the garments impeded the movements of the troops as they advanced, but under the crackling orders of officers similarly clad they swarmed upon the slope of the span—toward the leveled guns of the enemy, into the snarling thunder of the invader's tanks.

Crashing gun-fire broke the silent dawn in New York. The high-speed weapons in the turrets of the raiding tanks sprayed out fire and lead. Hailing death struck among the United States troops as they came, a desperate column steadily mounting the bridge. Scores fell under the first terrific blasts of the guns. The highest peak of the span rapidly became a No-Man's Land across which lethal lead whistled.

At the moment the infantry first struck, other detachments poured into the Holland Tunnel as well as the railway shafts beneath the Hudson. In each, the over-coated army met a wall of mailed troops. The clattering of crawling tanks mixed with the deafening din of rifles and high-speed machine guns. The middle of each tube became an embattled frontier.

ON THE river a few unwieldy ferry-boats which had been docked on the Jersey side of the Hudson pushed toward the Manhattan piers. The guns of the infantrymen crowding their decks turned fusillades upon the black-backed crowding submarines ominously maneuvering to block their advance. On the superstructures of the underwater monsters, machine-guns burst into action, fountaining death toward the unprotected ferries. The raging of the battle on the bridge and the fury of the conflict on the water became blanketed away as the thundering power of driving torpedoes struck.

Terrific explosions blasted the ferries out of the water. Blinding flame sprang up as the American forces were catapulted into the river, scores instantly killed, or mangled and dying. The boats became broken wreckage scattered on reddened waves while the submarine guns continued to blast death upon frantic men struggling in the water. Slugs hailed down on those stunned by the shock, rendered helpless by the very electrical equipment which had been designed to save them. The Hudson became a crimson stream of carnage.

Beyond the Bay, the naval unit of the counter-attack went swiftly into action. The battleships of the United States Scout Squadron had crept dose to the city under cover of darkness. Officers had taken their bearings with the most painstaking care; the big guns had raised their snouts upon carefully calculated marks. Blasting thunder rocked the sea and screaming shells arced in their trajectories. Into the Hudson, the fury of the counter-attack struck…!

Projectiles screamed down and blinding fire sprang up with swelling clouds of fumes. The water churned in turmoil around the slinking subs the naval guns were striving to hit, while under-water craft darted swiftly along the jutting piers, launching torpedoes at the embattled ferries as they prepared to dive. The cannonade quickened and the storm of battle broke more savagely over the river while torpedoes stopped the infantry attempting to cross the river. As the battle reached its height, the oil of submarines, like the blood of wounded sea mammoths, spread over the river. The remaining craft of the under-sea flotilla plunged beneath the surface—driving toward the bay and the battleships of the Scout Squadron.

The first gleam of the sun flashed off the wings of soaring army and navy bombers. The onslaught of the air squadrons was timed to the very instant the infantry first dashed with the enemy—when the first shells screamed from the cannon in the bay. The howling formations swooped low while observers searched the water for the outlines of submarines. Others hurled themselves toward the mailed troops massing on the giant span. Out of the sky bombs came streaking.

Along Riverside Drive, anti-aircraft batteries went swiftly into action. Their uncanny range-finders aimed the lifted barrels upon the flying cordons of the United States counter-attack. Even as high explosives plummeted upon the mailed invaders, shrieking shrapnel rained upon the American battle birds. Riddled bombers plunged with dead men in their pits as others wheeled in a desperate effort to bombard the archie concentration.

A fierce hope of victory filled the hearts of the United States commanders when their armed power struck—but suddenly, in the midst of the raging warfare, the cold came…!

IT CAME swiftly, bringing a piercing bitterness into the air, enveloping both the city and the surrounding water, spreading over the American forces with a dread, devastating power. At its first sharp pinch, the crackling orders of the United States officers demanded the use of the electrically heated garments. On the bridge, in the under-river tubes, on the battleships, and in the swirling planes, men connected their batteries to the resistance coils sewn inside their heavy coats. Warmth came to them, justifying a hope that the garments would save them from the ravages of the cold. But as the penetrating chill in the air grew sharper, the devices seemed not to function at all. The cold bit through despite the protection, and pierced with numbing intensity the hearts of the United States fighters.

Snow appeared in the air like a bursting cloud, swirling on Arctic winds. It came blindingly thick as the cold augmented swiftly. Hope of victory for the invading American forces gave way to dread and terror as the deadly cold struck.

THE CLOUDING white on the Hudson blanketed a powerboat which shot out from a hidden point on the Jersey shore. Operator 5, crouched at the helm with S-12 and Tim Donovan behind him, strove to force the boat through the raging of the storm. The savagely tossing water was strewn with the wreckage of destroyed ferries, with the fragments of fallen planes, with soldiers who had died before the frightful onslaught of the enemy machine guns and torpedoes.

Through gathering ice. Operator 5 plunged the power-boat northward. Fearing that the raiders had posted themselves at every pier, that even his private boat-house in the East River had been seized, he gambled on reaching a point in the Harlem River where the invaders might be less vigilant. He kept close to the Jersey shore, then swung sharply against the savagery of the storm, and drove across the river. The thunder of battle continued behind him as he sent the craft darting through blinding snow and under a railroad bridge. Undercover of the clouding white, he swerved alongside an abandoned houseboat which clustered among others—a Negro colony—at the water's edge.

The punishing cold made their movements an ordeal as Jimmy Christopher, Tim Donovan and S-12 scrambled from the boat. The street was heaping with white as they hurried along it, searching every window and doorway against the possibility of discovery by the mailed troopers. They drew their coats tight and leaned against the shrieking wind as they struggled through the mounting drifts.

"Keep with me!" Operator 5 warned through the raging of the storm and the rumbling of the battle. "The Intelligence maintains a garage near here—the invaders may not have found it!" He turned a corner as he spoke, and at the intersection beyond saw squads of mailed men running—a parade of monster tanks speeding to throw their power against the American counter-attack. "We've got to get under cover!"

OPERATOR 5 longed into a drifted doorway, peered around

sharply, and attempted to listen through the stormy bedlam. This was the entrance to the secret Intelligence garage; but, blinded by the storm, he could not determine whether the invaders had taken possession of it yet. With numbed hand, he thrust a key into the lock and chanced an entrance.

Tim Donovan and S-12 came to a shivering, gasping stop behind him. They stood in a dark, brick passageway. Operator 5's alert eyes peered along its length as they listened warily. The walls subdued the screaming of the storm and the concussions of the battle; but the cold had crept through. With their coats and their gloves affording them scant protection, they stole along the corridor.

The cavernous room they entered housed six powerful sedans—part of the fleet assigned to the Intelligence in New York. Jimmy Christopher saw that the massive bars on the broad doors were in place; some measure of relief came to him as he realized that the invaders bad not penetrated to this station. He crossed quickly to a small, partitioned office in the far corner and grasped the telephone.

Operator 5 waited in torture for an answer on the line which he knew was not connected with the public telephone system; it was part of the secret web of Intelligence wires. His heart speeded when, at last a faint click sounded and an almost inaudible voice followed.

"Operator 5 reporting!" Jimmy Christopher exclaimed. "Can you hear me? Connect me with W-8!"

"Louder—speak louder!" came faintly over the wire. "The cold is putting the line out of commission!"

Jimmy Christopher shouted into the transmitter, and was rewarded with: "W-8 is here!"

The voice of the New York chief followed quickly: "Operator 5! Thank God you've succeeded in getting into the city! BM flashed us a code report that you planned to attempt it For God's sake, watch yourself! The city is swarming with troops and with secret police."

"Have you any information concerning the headquarters of the invaders in the Vertex Building?" Operator 5 asked while his fear increased that the line would cease functioning at any moment.

"Operator H-3 has been detailed to cover that position," W-8 sang back. "His report has not yet come through. He will make use of the telephone at Station 66 at exactly noon. If you can manage it, you had best attempt to contact him personally there."

THE VOICE of W-8 faded into nothingness as Operator 5 strove to hear the last words. He called anxiously over the line, but there was no answer. The same frightful cold that was paralyzing his body had sapped the electrical energy from the fine. It meant that the cold-force had isolated TS-NY from its only means of communicating with the Intelligence men indie field.

Jimmy Christopher lurched from the booth and desperately ran back and forth in the garage with S-12 and Tim Donovan. Outside the brick walls, the shrieking of the wind had subsided. The white death was closing down on the city and the army and navy forces with even cruder intensity. A heavy dread weighted the heart of Operator 5 as he vainly tried, by exercising, to instill some degree of warmth into his aching body.

He struggled again into the partitioned space, turned the cock of gas-heater and fumbled with a match. Even the flame was subdued by the intensity of the cold and the gas, when it ignited at last, burned with a low, feeble flame that radiated scant warmth. Jimmy Christopher and his companions hovered around it miserably, listening to the rumble of the battle outside.

"Our attempt to retake New York cannot possibly succeed now!"

Tragic annihilation bad swept through the forces of the United States. The mailed troops of the invaders had advanced inexorably across the gigantic span on the Hudson. Their metal-scaled uniforms protected them completely from the cold as they pushed mercilessly against the crushed American infantry. In the hard-packed white on the bridge, hundreds of soldiers lay frozen. Blots of red marked the snow over which the stricken army was forced to retreat. Men dropped exhausted, victims of the freezing death, during that tragic retreat.

The crews of the American tanks found themselves trapped among the horde of the mailed men as their motors failed and steel machinery cracked apart like brittle glass. Imprisoned within walls of steel which could not keep out the cold, they became frosted corpses.

In the air, the cold became a destructive power far more terrible than the vicious blasting of the invaders' anti-aircraft batteries. As power-plants failed, planes plunged toward the white-caked river with pilots and observers frozen in the pits. Each craft shattered to bits as it struck.

The power of the cold, as it sharpened, extended over the

Bay and struck paralysis upon the Scout Squadron. While a few observers managed to remain in the air—while wireless messages were still able to flash through that stultifying cold—officers battled desperately to continue the attack. The gun-crews were scarcely able to move as they rammed projectiles and powder bags into the breeches of the cannon. And when that tortuous task was accomplished, the command of "Fire!" brought added horror.

Blasting explosions rocked the ships. Projectiles jammed in the barrels shrunken by the cold, and a devastating backfire smashed the turrets and the crews to bits. The frightfulness of the disaster left the ships staggering in a sea that was rapidly thickening with ice. Engines ceased to function as frantic commanders ordered withdrawal. Inexorably, relentlessly, the cold brought doom, turning the battle boats into argosies of the dead, trapped in a glacial sea....

Then, as mysteriously as it had come, the cold began to alleviate. As the temperature slowly rose, the forces of the enemy returned to their impassable frontier. On all the bridges, on all the roads, tanks and mailed troops maintained the isolation of the island. In the river, the sleek-backed submarines reappeared, guns bristling from their superstructures. The enemy ring remained unbroken around New York....

With the lifting of the cold, the secret wires of the Intelligence began to function once more. In BM, the President and Z-7 had been waiting in agonized suspense for the first flash from the battle front. When it came, it filled them with despair—a brief line of black letters on a yellow flimsy:

PROFOUNDLY REGRET UNITED STATES FORCES UTTERLY ANNIHILATED. FALK.

ON THE desk lay other reports which had been flashed into BM during the siege of New York. Each had struck horror into the hearts of the President and Z-7—each revealed the descent of the cold force on other cities. Devastating storms were playing over Seattle and Los Angeles, howling down on Denver and Cleveland, opening a new point of attack across the Mexican border at El Paso. Like scattered outbreaks of a virulent infection, the forces of invasion were springing up to win position after position on United States soil. The strength of the raiders had multiplied—while the first desperate attempt to drive them from the country had disastrously failed!

Z-7's eyes gleamed as he read another message that came clicking slowly out of a teletype receiver. The president read it with tightening lips. They gazed at each other wordlessly, scarcely daring to express their fervent hope. The report read tersely:

… BM… SPECIAL… OPERATOR 5 HAS SAFELY REACHED NEW YORK… TS-NY….

CHAPTER 7
BEHIND SECRET WALLS

A S HIGH noon neared, a cold sun glared upon the frosted spire of the famed Vertex Building in mid-Manhattan. Around it the mailed invaders had established guarded barricades. The streets and avenues lay almost impassable under the new deluge of snow, while mighty tanks guarded the tramped lanes which wound past the mountainous drifts, with guns constantly swinging. Metal-clad sentries patrolled the entrances to the building. It bad been changed to a towering fort by the ruthless raiders.

Operator 5, trudging along a footpath, his numb hand closed around the automatic concealed in the pocket of his heavy coat, peered intently at the barricaded zone. Fifth Avenue had become a canyon of sloping, white walls. Every store was banked high and deserted. In the hotels and apartments along the side-streets, he knew, some of the thousands crushed under the invasion were desperately trying to warm themselves. He paused near the menacing tanks as he heard the purr of a motor behind him.

A parade of heavy cars, their tire-chains rattling, was approaching the Vertex Building. Those which headed the procession, and others which brought up the rear, were open and filled with troops garbed in glittering uniforms of metal scales. Their rifles, covering the street, protected the occupants of the two closed cars even after they passed the barricades. The men who climbed from the sedans, as Jimmy Christopher watched, were also garbed in uniforms of mail, but golden decorations on their shoulders and helmets disclosed them to be officers of the invading command.

The massive man who strode first into the entrance of the rearing building was a dominating individual whom the mailed troopers saluted smartly as he passed with quick, strong strides.

Though he had glimpsed only his icy, merciless eyes, Operator 5 knew with grim satisfaction that he had seen the supreme commander of the enemy forces—Commissar Evol Kran.

Jimmy Christopher turned from the guarded area, wound his way past the mounted snow-drifts in the side-street. He entered the lobby of a hotel where only candles were burning, for the enemy controlling the power plants had cut off all master switches except those serving their own purposes. On the third floor, he knocked at a door; hearing no answer, he admitted himself with a key.

He entered a room which was bare, save for a table and a telephone. Four men, who had been moving about painfully in an attempt to combat the cold, paused as Operator 5 faced them. He recognized them as members of the New York unit of the Intelligence. He displayed his credentials; they scanned his eyes hopefully. One designated U-11 blurted:

"You've hung up a record better than any other man in the service, Operator 5—but this time you're helpless too!"

"It's only a matter of time," E-3 declared, "until every one of us is tracked down and shot. It's happened already. I've seen my best friend shot down in the street because he was known to the enemy as an Intelligence agent."

Operator 5 smiled tightly. "We still can't admit defeat. As long as we have any organization left we've got to use it as best we can. The failure of our counterattack this morning proves that the Intelligence is our only hope of breaking the war machine."

HIS QUIET firm tone brought reassurance to the suffering men in the frigid room. They did not speak while he took up the telephone. Like the instrument in the hidden garage, it was connected directly with the secret system centering in TS-NY. The voice that answered quavered with the cold, and Operator 5 immediately asked for W-8.

"Has H-3 reported, sir?" he inquired when the New York chief answered.

"Not yet. He is overdue. Operator 5, information for you has come through from BM. Agents still in Washington have managed to get word out that the passages beneath WDC-13 have not been reached by the enemy. Your prisoner is still being held in the cell there."

With grim satisfaction, Jimmy Christopher urged: "Ask BM to take every possible means of holding him, W-8. He may possibly become extremely valuable to us."

"BM reports that so far it has been impossible to penetrate into Washington, but they are attempting to open a way. Further information has come from Z-7 concerning the metal garment you smuggled out of Washington in your car. A government chemist has attempted an analysis of it but so far results are negligible. It consists of a metal inner—and outer-lining, separated by an ordinary wool fabric. But the composition of the alloy has not been determined, except that it is definitely radioactive."

"It is absolutely necessary that we discover the nature of the alloy," Operator 5 replied. "I'm certain that it's the radioactive element which provides protection against the cold.* Once we learn the composition, we may be able to fabricate uniforms of the same land for our own troops."

"I will get your report through at once," W-8 promised. "We are still keeping ourselves imprisoned in TS-NY, but I've had to inform Z-7 that we can't hold out much longer. We can't smuggle in enough food to keep us alive. Four of the men who were trapped in here with us have died of the cold. We're doing our damnedest to stick it out. But if this keeps up we'll turn into maniacs."

"Stay at your post at all costs, W-8!" Operator 5 urged. "H-3's report may give us some hope of reaching the enemy command." He glanced around as the door opened and a man with emaciated face shouldered in. "H-3 is here now. Stand by for his report!"

The lean undercover agent breathed heavily with exhaustion. He took the instrument from Jimmy Christopher's aching hand and exclaimed breathily: "Chief! I've been doing my best to find some means of tapping the enemy's line but it's impossible! They've set an impenetrable guard over every operation."

Operator 5's eyes reflected despair as he waited for H-3 to complete the discouraging report. At his gesture, the lean agent

---

* AUTHOR'S NOTE: In 1903, it was shown by Curie and Laborde that a radium compound was always hotter than the surrounding medium, and radiated heat at a constant rate. Measurements have been made of the heating effect of radium, uranium and thorium. This evolution of heat is enormous compared with that emitted by any other known chemical reaction.

followed him into the adjoining room. They faced each other grimly, H-3 in an agony of despondency, Jimmy Christopher still grimly determined to discover the weak point in the enemy's armor.

"You're the best man working under W-8, and I know you'd have results to report if it were possible to get them. Do you mean that there's absolutely no way of learning what the enemy's moves will be?"

"None!" H-3 exclaimed: "Their headquarters is so closely guarded that no one except officers in high command can get past the barricades without a special pass signed by Commissar Kran. Every inch of the communicating system is guarded constantly. I've made two attempts to break through, and they've cost us six of our best men!"

H-3 rapidly related his activities.

"They hunt us down like animals!" he rushed on. "They know the identity of most of our agents—and every one of us is a marked man. I've seen three of the best operators in this area shot down in cold blood by the secret police. I know that at least a dozen more have been killed by firing-squads without even the formality of a court-martial. God, we can't work against them when we're forced to hide for our lives."

"Somehow," Jimmy Christopher declared, "we've got to introduce an agent in the enemy's headquarters. We've got to reach Kran, somehow, and through him provide an opening for a new counter-attack. There is no other way to victory. If there is absolutely no hope that any agent in the service—"

"An utter impossibility," H-3 reiterated.

OPERATOR 5'S eyes darkened thoughtfully. As he turned back to the door, he heard a new voice in the next room—a woman's. He caught the words: "Now, or it will be too late!" followed by an anxious: "I'll take you there!" in the tones of F-17. Operator 5 entered the room just as the outer door closed. Before it was shut, he glimpsed the strikingly beautiful face of a young woman framed against a mink collar. Alertly he asked: "Who was that?"

D-14 answered: "Operator M-10. F-17 is taking her to TS-NY."

"What?" Jimmy Christopher asked in surprise. "An agent in this area who doesn't know the location of the Manhattan head-quarters? Are you sure of her, D-14? That's highly important!"

"I've never seen her before, but she showed us her credentials. She said that she works out of PHP in Philadelphia, and was caught by the invasion before she could report back. She showed us a cipher message—"

Operator 5 lifted the telephone quickly, rattled the hook. "Connect me with W-81" be urged as D-14 hurried on:

"A message she couldn't decipher—she thinks it's a dispatch connected somehow with the invasion. Because it might be important she insisted on being taken—"

"W-8!" Jimmy Christopher clicked into the transmitter. "Have you a record of Operator M-10, a woman, working out of PHP? This information is vital."

"One moment Operator 5." He waited with burning impatience. "Yes, there is a woman designated M-10 working out of the Philadelphia office. She is twenty-five, brunette, very pretty, blue eyes, height—"

Jimmy Christopher's ejaculation silenced W-8. He turned swiftly from the telephone with his eyes gleaming. "M-10's eyes are blue, and this girl's are brown! It means her credentials are forged, and her cipher message is a trick. An espionage agent of the enemy! We've done our utmost to keep the location of TS-NY a secret—and F-17 is leading her there now!"

He snapped open the door as he spoke. He rushed through the candle-lighted lobby, into the snow-heaped street, to see a sedan winding its way across town. Its direction left no doubt in Jimmy Christopher's mind that it was heading directly for TS-NY. As he glimpsed it, he saw another car swing around a corner to follow it. Through the windows of the second he caught the glitter of uniforms.

"Enemy officers!" Operator 5 blurted.

H-3 exclaimed: "My car's here!"

They hurried past a huge drift, to the coupé parked beyond. As Operator 5 slid to the wheel, H-3 unlocked the ignition. The motor was hot and caught at once. Jimmy Christopher sent it sliding into the narrow lane between the drifts while its wheels spun. Because it would be impossible to pass the enemy car in order to reach F-17 and the woman, he was forced to twist into the avenue. At the next cross-street he turned again in the first direction and urged the motor to its limit.

He was certain now that the woman's subterfuge was direct at learning the location of TS-NY; he knew that the only hope of defeating the plan lay in heading off F-17 before the hidden headquarters was reached. When he swung again, into the street on which TS-NY was located, he saw F-17's car twisting to a stop near the banked curb.

HE GLIMPSED the enemy officers following behind as he sprang from the wheel. Through the windshield of the sedan, one mailed figure was visible, raising a microphone to his hooded face. Operator 5 realized instantly that the car was equipped with wireless; that information was already flashing back to the enemy headquarters. In dismay, he fought past a huge drift, toward the cleared doorway which F-17 and the woman were approaching. The girl stopped as they reached it turned on the Intelligence man with a derisive laugh.

"Now we have learned!"

Operator 5's automatic was leveled in his gloved hand when he came to a stop. The glint of the weapon and the grim light in his eyes forced the contemptuous smile from the red lips of the woman spy. He said crisply: "Consider yourself my prisoner."

Again the woman laughed scornfully. Jimmy Christopher saw that the officers' car was stopping, that the mailed figures were springing from it. Automatics were gripped in their glittering fists as they began moving toward the door which led into the hidden Intelligence headquarters. Desperately H-3 fired; his bullet started a staggering attack from the invaders' guns.

Reports cracked in rapid succession as Operator 5 gripped the arm of the woman espionage agent. He forced her away from the door. F-17, overwhelmed with dismay, backed into the doorway as bullets splintered into the door. Jimmy Christopher thrust the woman into the narrow lane of the street, toward the coupé. As the onslaught of the invaders' guns sent slashing bullets at him, H-3 staggered against the sloping wall of snow, and crimson marked it.

"Get clear!" he gasped at Operator 5. "Get away from those devils."

Jimmy Christopher thrust the woman toward the car, into it. His thumbs pressed hard to a point behind her temples as she fought to escape him. The jiu-jitsu tactic sent the woman sagging to the seat. Swiftly, Operator 5 meshed the gears and sent the coupé lurching away.

A fresh fusillade of lead barked from the guns of the enemy officers. Bullets clanged against Jimmy Christopher's machine as he careened along the narrow lane. The woman lay motionless beside him as he frantically twisted the wheel to keep the car from plunging into the drifted snow. The blasting attack continued until he swung past the corner. His last glimpse of the embattled street showed him mailed officers charging at the scarred door, with F-17 and H-3 lying on crimson-splotched snow.

High in the Vertex Building, in Commissar Kran's headquarters, a captain clad in mail clicked the cam of a dictograph: "An important message, sir!" He strode through a connecting door, toward a massive desk at which a huge man sat in resplendent uniform. With a click of heels and a snappy salute, the Captain informed Commissar Kran: "The New York headquarters of the Intelligence has been located, sir!"

The blunt fingers of the invading commander drummed on

the desk. He peered piercingly at the Captain as though he had not heard. His voice was a chesty rumble as he said:

"The message is not from my son. You would have informed me at once if it were."

"No, sir. There is still no word from Major Kran."

The heavy fist of Commissar Kran slammed to the desk. "He must be found! Instruct General Urdick at Washington that at all costs my son must be found. Those are his special orders. He is personally responsible. Unless General Urdick finds my son, I will have him shot!"

The captain's face blanched. "Yes, sir! This message, sir. The address of the New York Intelligence."

Commissar Kran turned glaring eyes on the scrawled words. His voice became a savage, grating snarl. "Why do you occupy me with this trivial matter? There is but one order to give. Destroy it! Destroy that Intelligence office at once!"

"It will be done immediately, sir."

The captain withdrew hastily from the menacing presence of the Commissar. At his desk, he swiftly wrote detailed orders; and when the message reached the radio room, bearing the imposing signature of Commissar Kran, it flashed into the ether.

At the Battery, an officer received the orders through the field receiver. His crackling commands snapped the gun crew into action. Mailed men moved with mechanical precision to adjust the range of the piece. It was already loaded; once its aim was checked, a crashing explosion flung through the sky a projectile loaded with doom for the suffering Intelligence men in TS-NY....

CHAPTER 8
MINION OF DOOM

A FROSTED coupé lurched to a stop in a snow-piled canyon of the East Forties in Manhattan while leaping flames, visible across the city, still signaled the annihilation of TS-NY. The mounded, white doorways had been cleared so that the suffering families in the block might reach the stores for the scant rations allowed them by the omnipotent invaders. Toward one of these modest brownstone houses the driver of the car ventured.

Jimmy Christopher warily searched the street as he unlocked the door of the house designated Address Y in the lexicon of the destroyed Intelligence. Leaving it ajar, he turned back at once, making sure that he was not being watched. Quickly, he lifted the unconscious woman espionage agent into his arms. As he hastened toward the door with her, it was swung wide by the surprised Tim Donovan.

Operator 5's orders had sent the boy and S-12 here from the hidden garage station. Tim had been waiting anxiously for his friend's return. Now he closed the door tightly as Jimmy Christopher climbed the stairs toward the living room.

As Operator 5 hurried across the living-room with the unconscious woman in his arms, a mild-mannered man and a very pretty girl hurried toward him. Too startled to speak, pinched by the cold, they followed him into an adjoining room. There he lowered the spy to a bed. He peered intently from her lax face to that of the bewildered girl who was gazing at him.

"Jimmy—what's happened?" Diane Elliot asked.

Operator 5's hand closed on hers snugly. Months ago he had met Diane in the midst of a very trying case. They had become fast friends, and she had helped him signally in many of his most important details. Her ability had won her a position as special writer for the far-flung Amalgamated Press news service, but she had again and again subordinated her hunger for sensational news to Operator 5's necessity of complete secrecy in his under-cover work. As she searched his eyes now, she sensed a desperate plan of action forming in his alert mind.

"This woman," he declared, "is responsible for the destruction of the New York Intelligence headquarters. We've got to keep her prisoner here. Diane, are you willing to run a dangerous risk for me—as our only hope of reaching the invading command?"

"You know I'll do anything in the world you ask of me, Jimmy," the girl answered promptly. "We've been forced to hide here like hunted animals ever since the raiding began. Nothing matters now but driving the enemy out—somehow."

Operator 5 directed quickly: "Diane, this woman will regain consciousness within an hour. I want you to study her face—every line of it. Its shape and pigmentation are almost the same as yours. Make use of everything I've taught you about disguise, and transform yourself into that woman as closely as possible. Will you do that, Di?"

"I'll try my best, Jimmy!"

JIMMY CHRISTOPHER quickly searched the pockets of the captive's coat as well as her muff. With her purse in his hands, he withdrew from the room, leaving Diane to examine her face.

John Christopher, the father of Operator 5, had once been designated Operator Q-6 in the United States Intelligence. Years ago, a serious wound had forced him to retire from the Service. Two bullets lay so close to his heart that no surgeon dared remove them; they constantly threatened him with death. Yet cautioned to avoid all strain, he continually tried to assist his son in several perilous cases. Now he said quietly as he watched his son's eyes darken with thought: "If there is anything I can do to help, Jimmy, you know you can count on me."

"I know, Dad. And we need every man now. Without a head-quarters to direct us—with every agent hunted by the secret police of the invaders—we've got to try to establish a new central office. This is the only possible place—you're the man to take W-8's place. We'll plan it later."

He carried the woman spy's purse into his work-rooms at the rear of the house. They were filled with strange apparatus of which only Operator 5 knew the nature; each of the many shelves were loaded with experimental devices. Here Jimmy Christopher undertook chemical and electrical researches, constructed ingenious tools for himself, and originated the feats of magic with which he continually amazed Tim Donovan. He sat at a desk, emptied the woman's purse, and examined its contents closely.

The cipher message, by which she had tricked F-17 into betraying the location of TS-NY, engaged his attention for many minutes. He concluded that it was meaningless, put it aside. Finding nothing else of interest, he closely examined the purse. A quiet exclamation of satisfaction passed his lips as be discovered the opening of a secret pocket in the lining. From it, he brought a card and a folded bit of paper.

Sight of the card galvanized him. It bore a few printed lines in a foreign language, and the name of Kada Aldee. Beneath the printed designation, ZZ-33, was the heavily scrawled signature of Commissar Evol Kran. Operator 5 carefully noted the watermark, the impressive embossed stamp centered around the initial K, and murmured:

"Her credentials as one of the enemy's secret police!"

He studied the cryptic message on the slip of paper intently. He recognized it at once as a clever substitution cipher which avoided repetition of letters. His first work for the United States had been in the service of MI-8, the Codes and Ciphers division of the Military Intelligence during the World War, under the direction of Major Herbert Yardley. His astounding ability to decipher secret messages now stood him in good stead. He worked quickly, applied tests which he had devised, and found a clue....

HIS PENCIL skipped over a pad, writing the terse translation of the message, and his eyes gleamed:

Kada Aldee:—Your valuable services to the Secret Police have raised you even higher in my esteem. Once we have established ourselves, present yourself to me at our headquarters for special recognition of your services. This message will serve as your pass. Kran.

117

Operator 5's fist hit the desk with a triumphant thump. "She did not make use of it! Now we will!" He looked up to ask: "Diane—?"

"She's locked herself in the other room, Jimmy," Tim Donovan answered.

Operator 5 rose, brought special paper and ink from a compartment. He studied the credential card of Kada Aldee, and began to work quickly. He molded plastine over the embossed stamp, then quickly mixed a small quantity of sculptor's plaster of paris and made a cast of the impression. While it hardened, he dipped a brush in a special wax solution and, with deft strokes, imitated the watermark of the woman spy's card on his own. With finest India ink and a needle-pointed pen he reproduced the heavy printing. With another, he wrote in the name of Endo Orvello, and the designation of ZZ-42.

With the utmost care he reproduced the heavy scrawl of Commissar Kran's signature. At last, when the ink was dry, he pressed the card over the plaster cast and, with a pointed stick, forcing the fibers of the card into the pattern, reproduced the embossed stamp. When he rose, he had created a credential card exactly the same as the woman spy's except for the name and designation.

"You, S-12," he declared cryptically, "have become Endo Orvello of the enemy's secret police. My plan is not complete, but—"

As his voice faded, John Christopher asked quietly: "What nation is responsible for pillaging our cities? It's the most stupendous international crime in history. Who are the invaders?"

"It is not any one nation, Dad," Jimmy Christopher explained. "All the world powers are organized against us. Kran's fatherland—and that of any of the officers—does not matter. They've created a gigantic super-nation actuated by one desire—to subjugate and eliminate us as the controlling factor in international affairs."

Jimmy Christopher explained that for long months the world powers had been preparing for war, arming themselves more powerfully than ever before; and even the United States had joined in this armament race with a gigantic military program. Unarmed, the United States was a formidable enough element in any grave world situation; armed, she became a terribly dangerous uncertainty.

Treaties had been drawn up by these very nations, repudiated, rewritten, on all hands, until none could be sure of her allies or her enemies in the event of the outbreak of a new World War. Each nation knew that the United States could not keep out of that war when it broke, and that America's move, once it was made, would decide defeat or victory....

OPERATOR 5 moved nervously back and forth while his mind pieced together the fragments of a growing plan. His face became drawn, his eyes haggard, as he struggled with the dangerous problem. There was only silence in the room in which Diane had locked herself with the woman spy. Jimmy Christopher could not forget that this move entailed grave peril for the girl.

As he sank exhausted into a chair, Tim Donovan spoke quietly. "You've been concentrating on your job so hard, Jimmy—maybe you're losing your perspective. Maybe it'd help to get your mind off it for a few minutes. You've got some new tricks to show me, haven't you, Jimmy?"

Operator 5 smiled. "I think you're right, Tim. I've always got a new trick up my sleeve for you, old timer. Here's one right here that'll keep you guessing. Let's try it."

"Sure, Jimmy!" the boy exclaimed eagerly. "Whenever you show me a trick, I'm absolutely stumped, but the explanation is always mighty simple. It'll be that way with your job—wait and see."

"Okay, Tim." Operator 5 had taken a deck of cards from the desk. "We have a woman spy in this war game, so let's let this queen represent her. I want you to handle all the rest of the trick yourself, to eliminate the possibility of my putting something over on you. First, select two other cards—any two. Then, here are three small coin-envelopes you're going to use."

The boy took two cards at random from the deck, and, at Operator 5's direction, placed each of the three, including the queen, in one of the coin envelopes. They fitted snugly. Jimmy Christopher then directed the boy to leave the envelopes unsealed, but to place them behind his back and shuffle them so that the one containing the queen was mixed haphazardly with the other two. This done, the boy placed them in front of Operator 5.

"I'll try to select the envelope containing the queen," he exclaimed. "Of course, the envelopes are all exactly alike, and I certainly can't see through the paper. Not even you know which one contains the queen, do you, Tim? But by passing each one through my hand, and by calling on the powers of divination— yes!" Operator 5 had lifted each envelope in his fingers, and now he tossed one aside. "That's the queen!"

TIM DONOVAN quickly slid the card from the selected envelope and, to his amazement, found that it indeed contained the queen.

"Gosh, I don't see how you do that, Jimmy!" he exclaimed. "There's no difference in the envelopes; the cards all came from the same deck. You didn't get a glimpse of them once I closed the flaps. Can you do it again?"

"As many times as you wish, Tim."

He made his word good by repeating the trick six times. The Irish lad took every precaution to defeat Operator 5, by changing the cards in the envelopes, by shuffling them thoroughly, by watching Jimmy Christopher's every move, but he was completely baffled. Each time, Operator 5 unerringly selected the envelope containing the queen. Tim's painstaking examination of the cards and the envelopes disclosed not the slightest clue to the secret.

"I'd certainly like to know how you do it Jimmy!" he exclaimed.

"Let me show you another, first, Tim, before I explain this one," Operator 5 urged. "We'll use the same three cards, and three others." He took a trio of cards from the deck as he spoke, and placed all six face down on the table in a rectangle. "Now, while my back is turned and you're sure I can't see what you're doing, merely lift one of the cards, look at it, and replace it in exactly the same position."

Tim complied while Operator 5 turned to the wall. The card the boy glanced at was the ten of diamonds. He took great care to return it to its former position. Yet when Jimmy Christopher turned back, he immediately lifted the ten of diamonds and declared: "That's your card."

"Doggone!" Tim exclaimed. "You couldn't have seen me look at it and I know you couldn't tell from their positions which one I looked at. Let me try to figure it out while you do it again, Jimmy!"

"The first rule of a magician, Tim," Jimmy Christopher smiled, "is never to repeat a trick, but I'll break it for your sake, and even then I don't think you'll guess the answer. We'll try it as many times as you like."

Again he turned to the wall and again the boy glanced at a card. Though he replaced it carefully, in precisely the same position, Operator 5 immediately found it. Four more times the effect was produced, and Tim grew even more bewildered. Jimmy Christopher's face had lighted; he glanced eagerly at the door of Diane's room—as he heard a sound of movement and rapidly explained the secrets:

"In the first trick, with the queen, you failed to notice a slight difference in the cards, Tim. The whole secret is this—the queen is slightly narrower than the other cards. You see, when I prepared for the trick, I selected envelopes in which the cards fit snugly. I cut a very narrow margin off one edge of the queen with a sharp knife. Then I was all set.

"By holding the envelopes by their side edges, and squeezing just a little, the narrow queen can be detected inside the envelope, No matter what envelope it's in, you can always find it easily. The squeezing motion is so slight it isn't detected by the spectator, but it tells the magician exactly what he wants to know."

"That's a humdinger, Jimmy!" Tim exclaimed. "It certainly fooled me—and it's so easy to do, too!"

"As for the other," Operator 5 explained, "it's equally simple. Here, in the drawer of my desk, I have a small dish of ordinary salt. When I took up the deck, I also took up a pinch of the salt. Placing the cards on the table, I dropped a few grains on each card. You didn't notice that, of course, because the small grains are almost invisible—you can't see them unless you look for them.

"When you lifted your chosen card, naturally the grains of salt fell off. When I turned back, I had only to select the card from which the salt had been removed. The grains on the others told me immediately that they hadn't been touched. Of course, you use only a very small amount. All you need to do the trick once can be carried under your fingernail—but that's the whole secret!"

"You certainly had me stumped, Jimmy," Tim Donovan chuckled.

OPERATOR 5 turned as the door of the bedroom opened. His eyes widened at the young woman who appeared. She had the strikingly beautiful face of Kada Aldee, silhouetted against the mink collar of the spy's coat. She came to a pause just over the sill while the men in the room gazed in momentary consternation. It was Operator 5 who moved first, to stare through the open door, at the bed on which he had placed the unconscious woman....

He saw her lying there—the woman whose face was exactly like that of the girl standing in the doorway. She had been stripped of her outer clothing; her wrists and ankles were bound and she was gagged; consciousness had returned to her, and she was glaring through the doorway in cold fury.

The young woman in the doorway asked in the voice of Diane Elliot: "Do you think I will pass, Jimmy?"

"Excellent, Di!" Operator 5 exclaimed "Perfect! I thought, when you first stepped out, that you *were* Kada Aldee!"

Tim Donovan, John Christopher and S-12 murmured their amazement as Operator 5 closed the door. He drew the disguised girl away and spoke quietly. His eyes grew solemn as he said:

"Diane, this is the most dangerous job you've ever undertaken. There can be only one penalty if you are discovered. Commissar Kran will order your execution without the slightest hesitation if your disguise is discovered. I tell you this because you deserve the know the truth. Realizing that, Di—?"

"You know you can count on me, Jimmy," the girl answered levelly. "I'm not afraid!"

"Good girl! Your purpose, Di, is not only to get close to Kran—it's to learn of the enemy's system of communication and, if possible, the master strategy behind their scattered attacks."

"Yes, Jimmy!"

Operator 5 led the girl hurriedly into his workroom. "Here are your credentials. They will pass you into the headquarters." He brought a small metal device from a drawer of his desk. "This is a heliograph of special design. It contains batteries, a parabolic reflector and a small bulb which emits ultra-violet rays. This button on the side is a contact by which the light can be flashed in telegraphic code. It can send messages over a short distance—and it will be your only means of sending information out of the enemy headquarters."

"I understand, Jimmy."

"Understand this above all else," he insisted. "There is nothing more important than staying at your post. You've got to play the game through no matter what happens. Betray the Intelligence if you must. Turn upon S-12 without hesitation if the situation demands it. Even if it means the death of everyone dear to you, you've got to keep on being Kada Aldee; you've got to stay at the side of Commissar Kran and get your information out. Do you understand that? Do you?"

The distressed girl whispered: "Yes, Jimmy."

Operator 5 turned to the white-faced S-12. "This card identifies you as a member of the enemy's secret police. I've done my best to make it flawless, but it's possible they have some test which we can't foresee. If this deception is discovered, nothing can save you. You're going with Diane to protect her as far as possible. Protect her—understand? You must not hesitate to pay your life if it's necessary to maintain Diane's disguise in the enemy headquarters."

S-12 answered tightly: "I understand."

"You asked for an opportunity to redeem yourself," Jimmy Christopher reminded the undercover agent, "and this is your chance. You cannot permit yourself to fail."

"I won't fail."

Jimmy Christopher led the disguised girl and S-12 to the entrance of the house. He peered out on the snow-banked street, made sure it was empty, and took Diane's hand tightly in his. Impulsively she threw her arms about his shoulders; she crushed her hot lips to his. When she tore herself away, to hurry out the door, S-12 followed at her side.

Grimly Operator 5 watched the courageous girl begin her mission that promised a hope of salvation from the merciless invaders—or certain death…!

CHAPTER 9
RAIDERS' STRONGHOLD

A YOUNG woman in a mink coat, a young man with drawn face, boldly approached the military barricade established around the Vertex Building. Inside the armed lines, the streets had been cleared of snow. Mailed troopers were stationed at every approach, and at each entrance of the skyscraper. A score of tanks stood with running motors, their bristling turret-guns swung to cover every inch of the streets leading to the lofty headquarters of the invading forces. At a heavy chain which obstructed the street, Diane Elliot and S-12 paused, scrutinized by eyes gleaming piercingly through the goggles of a metal helmet.

Without speaking, they proffered their identification cards. The officer peered at them intently, and Diane winced for fear that his searching gaze would penetrate her disguise. He read aloud their cryptic designations, then scanned the cipher message which the girl handed him. Though its system made it extremely difficult to decipher by one not in possession of the key, the officer read it at a glance.

"You may pass, Kada Aldee," he declared gruffly through his metal hood, "but there is no mention here of your companion."

"Commissar Kran has received my information that I am bringing ZZ-42 with me," the girl answered firmly. "He has important data to report."

"Without a special pass—"

"You will admit him," the girl interrupted with a sharp ring in her voice, "or you will regret it! If you wish to risk punishment at the hands of Commissar Kran, very well—my companion will withdraw."

She saw the goggled eyes of the enemy officer narrow with a suggestion of terror. The mere hint of punishment from Kran filled him with dread. He carefully scanned the card which Operator 5 had so painstakingly forged; he shrugged and returned it.

"If it were not for your own message, I would not risk it Yet— why not? If this man has deluded you, if he is not what he seems, he will pay with his life. Pass!"

S-12 stepped forward at Diane Elliot's side, pallor creeping into his face. The elevator which carried them upward was operated by the gleaming hand of the enemy. Through office after office they passed, guard after guard, each step of the way an ordeal lest they betray themselves as they moved toward their destination. At last, they entered the adjutant's office, faced the door beyond which Kran's own office lay.

The walls of this room, of every room in the suite, were of the metal which repulsed the bitter cold. Beyond the door sounded the deep, rumbling voice of the Commissar, from whose merciless pronouncements there was no appeal....

WHILE DIANE Elliot and S-12 stood waiting, with the adjutant examining their credential cards, they heard the voice of another officer reporting information, and the chesty voice of Commissar Kran uttering his inexorable edicts.

The crash of a fist striking the desk carried through the connecting door. "Find him! Order all men now engaged on that detail in Washington be arrested and shot! Order Captain Arso to undertake a new search. Warn him that unless he brings my son to me within twenty-four hours, he too will die!"

"Yes, sir," the answer came very quietly. "Your signature to the dispatches, sir?"

"Our victory in the United States is a foregone conclusion, but it will mean nothing to me if Major Kran is not found!"

The connecting door snapped open; a pale officer strode away, carrying edicts, each bearing the heavy signature of the Commissar, each a sentence of doom. The adjutant at the desk briskly returned die credentials to Diane Elliot and S-12 as they stood grimly silent, and touched the cam of the dictograph.

"ZZ-33 and ZZ-42 reporting, Commissar."

"I will see them."

Diane's heart speeded as she faced the door of the supreme commander of the raiders. His stare was an ordeal as she advanced to the desk with S-12. He said: "You merit citation, Kada. You have justified my faith in you."

Diane ventured: "I have done my best, Commissar."

"Excellent—excellent. Due to your work, the New York headquarters of the Intelligence was wiped out of existence. I need you here, now. You will act as my adjutant to the secret police."

"Thank you, Commissar."

The great military genius spoke like an articulate machine. "Until the United States is completely crushed, until our victory is complete, your place will be here. Through you will pass the orders which will completely wipe out the United States Intelligence and establish our secret police in its stead. The zero hour—" The Commissar broke off as his piercing eyes turned to S-12. "Who is this?"

BEFORE DIANE could answer, a sharp knock sounded on the door and it opened. The adjutant entered swiftly, holding a record in one hand, and gazed sharply at S-12. He placed the document on the desk in front of the Commissar and said breathily: "Commissar, this woman and this man are impostors!"

A chill closed around the heart of Diane Elliot as she heard the words. She saw puzzlement in the eyes of Commissar Kran as he rose. A hush held in the room as his keen eyes searched her face, then turned to S-12. He spoke in a low, throaty tone that was a threat.

"Kada Aldee is known to me. I have known her since a child. If she vouches for this man?"

A report roared from S-12's gun just as Diane jarred his arm.

"Does she?" the adjutant asked quickly. "Does she vouch for him, Commissar?"

Diane Elliot was silent for one tortured moment. S-12

scarcely breathed. His backward glance showed him officers standing in the doorway with drawn guns. He could not move as Commissar Kran leaned forward with glinting eyes.

"What is your answer, Kada? Of you there is no doubt But this man with you—!"

She thought swiftly that Jimmy Christopher was depending upon her alone. She forced herself to smile, and to say, with a quiet firmness: "This man? I do not vouch for him. Commissar."

The adjutant burst out a mirthless laugh. "That is well! If you had, you would have signed your own death warrant. Your credentials are unquestionable, ZZ-33, but this man's are forged. If you had upheld him, you would have branded yourself a traitor!"

A repulsive surge flooded through Diane Elliot A death-warrant! She realized she had pronounced it on S-12. She heard, as if in a dream, the rumbling voice of Commissar Kran: "Forged?"

"Yes," Diane Elliot heard herself saying. "I know his credentials are forged. He represented himself to me as a member of our secret police, though I knew he was not. I allowed him to come here so that"—her voice faltered, but she steadied herself—"so that one more member of the United States Intelligence may be eliminated from the field."

"The Intelligence?" the adjutant snapped. "That man? In the American Intelligence?"

"Yes." Diane turned upon the wan S-12 and forced a mocking laugh. "He did not suspect that I led him here to die!"

"Excellent Kada!" Commissar Kran boomed. "Now, through him, we shall learn all the secrets of the American Intelligence.

Through him, we will gain information that will help us destroy it utterly. He will soon see what means we use to make our prisoners talk! Captain!"

"Yes, sir!"

"Put this man on the rack!"

PARALYZED WITH horror, Diane Elliot was only dimly aware of S-12's desperately swift movement. His hand flashed to his armpit holster. He spun with the weapon swinging toward the massive chest of Commissar Kran. The adjutant snatched frantically at his service automatic; the officers in the doorway crowded through, guns glinting in their hands. The finger of S-12 was tightening on the trigger when the frantic girl, driving herself to play the vital part assigned her by Operator 5, snatched at S-12's weapon.

She realized, even as she tore the gun down, that S-12 had deliberately delayed the shot so that she might seem to save the Commissar's life. A report roared as she struggled with S-12 and the bullet crashed to the side of Kran's desk. S-12 shouted: "Get back!" as be struck the girl away. She stumbled back, dazed by the blow, as he whirled toward the door. Instantly the automatics in the hands of officers near the door blazed.

Diane Elliot watched with terror in her heart as S-12 stumbled into the office beyond. The uniformed men sprang after him, their guns blasting out a deafening fusillade. Half a score of bullets tore into S-12's body as he backed. He staggered against one of the maps and smeared it with his ebbing life's-blood. He poised in torment, peering through the doorway, widened eyes upon the girl's. She saw him smile tightly, triumphantly, before he pitched headlong to the floor.

Bedlam filled the offices of Commissar Kran; but Diane Elliot stood motionless beside the commander's desk. Stung by grief, horrified at the grim necessity of what she had done, she watched the officers crowd around S-12. When the door shut and the adjutant turned back she heard distantly:

"We may thank Kada Aldee for your life, Commissar!"

Commissar Kran was breathing heavily, peering grimly at the girl. "My—my gratitude, Kada. For this, you shall receive the citation of the Black Ribbon. I am pleased to have one of your fortitude at my side. Excellent—excellent!"

The lips of Kada Aldee curved in a proud smile—but the heart of Diane Elliot beat chilled....

DARKNESS FILLED the snow-bound streets of the metropolis as a lone car crawled along the narrow lane of Madison Avenue. Night shrouded the besieged city in blackness, for the control of the power plants kept every window bleak, except in those areas chosen by the invaders. No other light save the gleam from the electric torches of the mailed troops, was visible. When the car crawled quietly to a stop in the gloom, two figures hurried out of it.

Operator 5 and Tim Donovan hastened to the door of a store which had not been in use since the first devastating blizzard. While the boy watched alertly, covering the footprints they had left in the snow, Jimmy Christopher tried one key after another in the lock of the entrance.

He had fashioned these implements in his workshop; they

were capable of opening any known type of lock. His fourth attempt withdrew the bolt, and he shouldered into thicker darkness. Tim Donovan followed.

They groped through a maze of furniture on display, and quietly mounted a flight of stairs. On the top floor, Operator 5 again used his keys to open a door leading to the roof. They shouldered against the packed snow and stepped out. Trudging through knee-deep white, sheltering themselves behind the housing, they peered at the frosted spire of the Vertex Building which rose less than a block away.

"There are troops stationed on every floor of that skyscraper, Tim," Operator 5 cautioned. "We may be spotted. But keep an eye on the windows."

"Trust me, Jimmy!"

"If I pick up any message from Diane, old-timer, transcribe it as I dictate."

"All set, Jimmy."

Operator 5 brought a pair of binoculars from his pocket and focused them on the Vertex tower. They were equipped with special filters which transformed the invisible wavelengths of ultra-violet light into frequencies visible to the eye. The device was the complementary part of the heliograph he had furnished Diane Elliot.

For long moments, he stood shivering in the snow, hoping to catch the flash of a message. He lowered his circles of vision to the windows below where, he knew, the enemy staff was quartered, and continued to search all the dark planes. Minutes dragged while Operator 5 maintained his position. Tim

Donovan crouched beside him, shivering, filled with impatience. Despair made Jimmy Christopher's heart heavy—until a reddish-blue sparkle appeared in one window.

"Ready, Tim!"

"She's signaling the numeral 5. Now it's beginning: 'So far—safe.' Don't miss a word, Tim. 'Appointed director—secret police—by Kran.' She's pressed now for time, Tim. It's coming in telegraphic short-hand. 'Communication maintained with other cities by confiscated telephone and telegraph systems as well as wireless. No message can be transmitted without Kran's signature. Violation of rule means death.'

" 'Preparing to subdue territory surrounding key areas. Reinforcements from the Mexican and Canadian borders deployed for new invasion. Troops now number hundreds of thousands. Master invasion-plan begins at midnight tomorrow.' "

Now the blinking blue-red gleam ceased; it resumed, but only after an interval.

" 'Kran ready to send forces to all seized cities midnight tomorrow lines will advance until controlled areas meet and entire nation is subjugated. Command considers success of this move infallible, for cold projectors will cover the advance. Entire country will be paralyzed by low temperatures and storm while invaders assume complete control of the country. Wait!' "

NOW THE high window was black, even through the lenses of Operator 5's filtering binoculars—a long, agonized interval while Jimmy Christopher kept staring. His fear grew that Diane had been forced to abandon her position when the weird blue-red spot reappeared.

"They've spotted us!" Machine guns sprayed lead at them!

"Coming again, Tim! 'Neutron projectors covering New York installed above headquarters in this building. Captain Rogiro, world-famed physicist, explained it. Electrical field slows atomic action. Beams of neutrons, penetrating all substances, absorb charges of atomic particles from all matter they permeate. Only means of combating cold is use of radioactive alloy of actinium, which radiates molecular heat Neutron projectors can produce cold almost as low as absolute zero and thus protect themselves against armed attack.'

"She's speeding up now, Tim," Operator 5 said. "She's pressed for time. Here's more: 'Kran is merciless machine except in attitude toward missing son. Love for son his only human quality. If you can—'"

Suddenly a blinding light stung Operator 5's eyes. In dismay, he jerked his glasses away to see the stabbing beam of a searchlight playing down from the observation platform at the very peak of the skyscraper. It was a dazzling brilliance that stunned Jimmy Christopher and shadowed his figure sharply against the white-heaped roof.

"They've spotted us!"

Swiftly, the tattoo of a machine-gun cut through the chill silence of the night. The withering attack hailed bullets on the roof as Operator 5 leaped down the narrow flight behind the boy.

As they sped down the stairs, he snatched the scrawled sheets from the boy's hand, thrust them into his coat pocket. They bounded down flight after flight and, once in the display room on the ground floor, sped toward the entrance. The shaft of the searchlight was sweeping into the white street, but the coupé lay in the shadow of the building. Operator 5 hurried to it as he heard crackling commands in the street beyond, and the first snarl of a moving tank.

He sent the car shooting ahead even as the Irish lad scrambled in. Instantly, machine-guns mounted on nearby buildings turned their muzzles upon the car and a thundering rain of lethal slugs beat down. Again, as Operator 5 plunged into thick darkness—once the machine-gun chorus subsided—he risked a slower speed to avoid the mailed troops posted along the avenues.

"They're flashing a radio alarm all over the city for us now, Tim—that's certain. We've got to abandon the car. Hop out, old-timer! There—into that restaurant!"

THE COUPÉ slid on the snow as the boy swung out to the running-board; it was still moving when he leaped off.

Hearing the snarling of a tank somewhere behind him, seeing mailed troopers gathering farther down the street—Operator 5 sprang toward a dim shine of light. He glanced back to see that the tumbling snow had completely covered the car, as he had hoped. He joined the breathless Tim Donovan in front of the small, candle-lighted restaurant.

"We've got to bluff it out, Tim!" Jimmy Christopher exclaimed in a whisper. "We may be caught—but if possible, we've got to get this information through to Z-7 at BM."

The advance of the tank and the troops forced them to hurry into the restaurant. It was one of the few in the city allowed to operate. Men in metal-scaled uniforms were posted inside it; they turned searching eyes upon every man and woman huddling at the tables, hungrily devouring cold food. Operator 5 and Tim Donovan were about to seat themselves when the door burst open and a mail-clad officer strode in heavily.

"Attention!"

A sharp chill seized Operator 5's heart as he realized he had in his pocket the transcript of the message which Diane had flashed. Their desperate retreat from the roof, their swift plunge along the white street their forced refuge in the restaurant, had given Jimmy Christopher no opportunity to hide it.

"Attention! Americans, there is a spy among you! There is a spy in this room!"

Jimmy Christopher's dread grew heavier as the officer advanced. Men and women had risen in terror from their tables; huddling in their coats, they blurted protests of innocence. Tim Donovan saw the whiteness of his friend's face, and he realized Jimmy Christopher's predicament He whispered, so softly that no one else could hear:

"Give them to me, Jimmy. If you don't, they'll find it on you and—"

"You will all be searched!" The Captain proclaimed it in sharp, accented syllables. "The spy must be found, or you will all suffer his penalty—you will all be shot! Speak up! Which of you is a secret agent of the enemy?"

THE MAILED men immediately turned with leveled guns on the men and women in the room. One confronted Operator 5, then stepped aside to a man and woman who stood terrified. Startled, Jimmy Christopher felt a slight movement beside him and realized, abruptly, that Tim Donovan's hand had slipped into his pocket and was withdrawing the folded papers.

Jimmy Christopher's breathy protest was stilled by a roaring: "Silence!" from the mailed trooper who swung to face them. A massive automatic leveled at Operator 5's heart, then pressed heavily against his body. A hand gloved in metal thrust into his pockets while he stood in anguish against the wall. The trooper turned away with a mutter, and pointed his weapon full upon Tim Donovan.

Operator 5 suppressed a moan of despair as an exclamation broke from the trooper's lips. He straightened with the folded sheets of paper in his hand. Instantly, the captain strode close, heels beating; he snatched the pages away, glared at them. Tim Donovan stood erect, his face white, as the eyes of the officer narrowed upon him through the thick lenses in his goggles.

"You are the spy! A boy—and a fool! No matter. You will face the firing-squad!" He bellowed with rage. "How did you get this information?"

Tim Donovan's lips curled scornfully. "Do you expect me to answer that?"

The officer stiffened. "The Commissar will learn of this at once. Perhaps"—his voice sharpened—"perhaps you are not alone on this mission." His gaze turned piercingly upon Operator 5. "Who is this man?"

The boy answered staunchly: "I don't know. I've never seen him before."

The trooper who had discovered the paper spoke gutturally.

"Perhaps he is lying, Captain. These two, they came into this place together."

"It just happened that he and I met at the door," Tim Donovan added quickly. "He knows nothing about it."

"So?" Still the officer peered at Operator 5. "Note his description," he ordered the trooper at his side. "I will flash it to headquarters at once. In the meantime," continued the officer to Operator 5, "you will be watched—and if this boy is lying to save you, you will face a firing squad with him!"

THE MAILED troopers gripped Tim Donovan's arms and jerked him away. Operator 5 saw the metal-clad men surround the courageous Irish lad; saw him take the first step toward execution by the merciless enemy. Tim marched unfalteringly toward the door, stepped out into the white-mounded street without one backward glance of betrayal....

Operator 5 waited during a moment of agony, listening to the tramp of the men who were escorting the boy away, and to the grinding of the tank as it wheeled and retreated. Realizing that now he was powerless to help Tim, he stepped into the street; but the squad was already gone; the boy was out of sight....

Again the war machine of the invaders functioned. The wireless equipment of the moving tank crackled out a message which flashed to the enemy's headquarters. The dispatch passed from hand to hand until the adjutant brought it to Commissar Kran. When he entered, he found the commander face to face with Kada Aldee. The captain snapped a salute and read the report briskly—and a glimmer of terror stole into Diane Elliot's eyes as she heard it.

"A spy has been apprehended, sir—a boy, carrying vital information. No explanation is given in the report of how he obtained it. I will search for the leak at once, sir. As for the boy?"

Mechanically, the Commissar uttered his usual edict: "Execute him at once."

In her overwhelming anguish, Diane Elliot risked an intervention. "Wait, Commissar. I think I know who this boy is."

"You know, Kada?"

"Yes. There is only one boy who might come into possession of vital information. His name is Tim Donovan. He is the unofficial assistant of Operator 5. Through him, we may learn of Operator 5's whereabouts in the city."

The Commissar studied her face intently while Diane struggled to conceal the anxiety she felt.

"Don't you understand?" she asked quickly. "If you withhold the order to execute the boy, we may be able to force him to talk. If we can trick him into betraying Operator 5, it will eliminate the Intelligence agent we most fear."

"True." Commissar Kran slapped the order to his desk. "Hold the boy prisoner. Torture will make him talk. An excellent idea, Kada!"

Diane Elliot winced; yet a fierce gladness filled her that even at this cost, she had stayed Tim Donovan's death.

"Perhaps, sir—this further information. A young man, seen with the boy just before he was made prisoner. This is his description. If the boy was lying, and he is connected somehow with the leak of information from this headquarters—"

Commissar Kran's fist crashed to the desk so violently that

the adjutant winced. "Fools! Imbeciles! This is a description of Operator 5, the very Intelligence agent we are seeking!" The Commissar rose heavily from his desk as Diane Elliot stared aghast. "Force that boy to talk at all costs—to reveal the leak in this headquarters! Order the men who are following Operator 5 to capture him! Flash them at once!"

CHAPTER 10
COUNTER-STRATEGY

O PERATOR 5 was a lone, dark figure moving along the snow-banked street. He had rapidly worked his way north on foot attempting to shake off the mailed men who were trailing him. His backward glance told him that in spite of all his efforts, the glimmering figures of the troopers were still dogging his steps. Anxiously, determined now upon a move which he hoped would shake them from their stealthy pursuit, he turned toward the entrance of a staid apartment-house near white-mounded Central Park, in the East Sixties.

A tank came snarling around the corner from Fifth Avenue as he neared the frosted door. A massive iron door on the side of it swung open and a mailed figure, decorated with the golden ornaments of a captain, sprang out of it. He called "Stop!" in a guttural, commanding tone as Jimmy Christopher began to push through the lobby. Operator 5's disobedience brought a slug crashing through the glass behind him; and at the sound of the report, he sped to the base of the stairs.

The captain, charging toward the shattered door, turned to shout at the running men who had been trailing Operator 5.

Jimmy Christopher heard heavy boots tramping up the stairs after him as he sped from landing to landing. On the eleventh floor, he hurried along a dark corridor and stopped breathless before a door. He unlocked it swiftly; he stepped into a small apartment.

The apartment was one he rented under the name of Huntley Walsh; he used it as a means of covering himself with a multiple identity. Hastily, he strode to a strange device bolted to a table anchored near the window. It consisted of a large drum around which a rope ladder was coiled, a ratchet, a powerful motor supplied by storage batteries banked in a closet and kept at full charge.

He brought it expertly into use as he heard pounding steel in the corridor and a chesty voice proclaim: "He went to that door—the snow tracks show it Break it open! He is in there!"

Jimmy Christopher hurriedly lowered forty feet of the rope ladder over the sill of the open window. He poised to climb out and heard a sharp hissing at the outer door. It told him that already the mailed troops were turning the greedy flame of an acetylene torch on the steel barrier. He quickly bolted the connecting door, then lowered himself on the ladder into a deep well of darkness.

He descended into a narrow cleft separating this building from the next; he swung to a small balcony. He could not avoid leaving tracks in the snow as he crawled over. The motor softly whirred when he let go of the ladder, the rope coiled upward past the sill, and the window above slid shut.

Shouldering through French windows, he crossed another small apartment and stepped into a corridor. Once past the turn, he touched a button inscribed: *Carleton Victor.* Almost at once the way was opened by a sharp-nosed, stiff-shouldered, immaculate manservant, who bowed and said with a suppressed shiver: "Good evening, Mr. Victor."

THE ESTIMABLE Crowe, gentleman's gentleman extraordinary, did not dream that Carleton Victor, photo-portraitist of world-wide reputation, was a convenient cover for Jimmy Christopher. Like the famous personages who considered it a privilege to sit before Victor's camera, the man-servant considered his master a great artist Though Crowe was sometimes baffled by Victor's eccentricities, his aplomb was never shaken, his cool poise never disturbed. Though he noticed now that Victor's manner was hurried and breathless, he permitted himself no curiosity.

"Crowe," Victor said imperatively, "I am not at home to any callers."

"Quite so, sir."

"If anything untoward should occur, Crowe, I will rely on your discretion."

"Certainly, sir."

Crowe's pointed nose twitched with concern as he followed Victor into the far rooms of the sumptuous, penthouse apartment. He was quite content, in his service to Victor, to make its four walls his entire world, but he had frequently wondered about one door at the end of the hall which his master kept constantly locked. He had never once been permitted a glance past it; he could not guess what strange secret it held. Now Victor approached it directly, slipped a key into the lock, and peered back as Crowe stiffened to respectful attention.

"That's all, Crowe."

"Certainly, sir."

Crowe watched Victor step quickly through the mysterious door, but glimpsed no detail beyond it. He could not know that, once past the sill, Victor was transformed into Operator 5.

A loud pounding at the entrance of the penthouse quickened Crowe's steps. The door was jarring in its frame as he indignantly opened the way. He peered out at strange figures—men garbed from head to foot in uniforms of mail, who peered at him threateningly through strange goggles. Yet even that did not shake his poise. With chastening reproach in his voice, he began: "There is a bell provided for—"

The leader of the mailed squad charged at Crowe as his men tramped into the apartment. Overwhelmed by their numbers, forced back against the wall in the face of a huge automatic, Crowe stood with pointed nose quivering with dismay; yet, his concern was not for himself, but for the disturbed privacy of his master. His aplomb was unruffled by the snarling demand of the captain of the squad:

"Where is Operator 5? He came here. Where is he, I say?"

"I don't understand," Crowe ventured. "You have evidently come to the wrong address. There is no operator of any denomination here. You will please leave at once!"

THE CAPTAIN laughed mockingly; he strode past Crowe, into the corridor after his men. They had already made a quick search of the library and bedrooms; and were gathering in front of the locked door through which Victor had disappeared "Break it down!" the commander snarled. Crowe repeated his protests but his very word was ignored. He stood back in dismay as the mailed squad attacked the closed door with heavy axes.

The panels splintered under the powerful blows. The captain charged into the room the instant the way was open. He strode through an empty space, peering at the dosed doors of small steel cabinets, which his men made sure were locked, raised a window, and peered down at a terrace three stories below. In the banked white the captain glimpsed fresh footprints.

"He's trying to get out of the building!"

The mailed troopers, led by their captain, swarmed into the lobby of the building and past the white-headed man in doorman's cloak who was piteously warming his blue-veined hands over the flame of a guttering candle. They ran into the street; they peered about but saw no sign of Operator 5. Since the silent guns of the waiting tank testified that their quarry had not shown himself, the captain turned back to the heavy-jowled doorman.

"Where is he? You must have seen him come down those stairs—you couldn't help it!"

In a quavering tone the doorman answered: "But I—I saw no one, sir."

The captain whirled with a snarl. "Search every floor, every apartment. Find Operator 5! Wherever he's hiding, drag him out and shoot him down!"

Again the troops swarmed into the building. The old door-man turned again to warm his palsied hands over the candle as mailed boots tramped the corridors. The grim raiders left no room untouched in their merciless search. They traced the movements of Operator 5 from the snow-packed terrace down the stairs, but there the trail vanished. When, at last, they gathered again in the lobby, their glittering eyes shone fiercely.

"No matter!" the captain snarled. "We'll keep watch on this building. We'll starve him out. Wherever he is, he is doomed!"

They strode out, posting themselves around the building. The doddering doorman continued to huddle over the candle. At last, with an old lunch-box under his arm, he went tottering along the white lane of the street. As he turned the corner, he glanced back to see the grim guards waiting alertly, guns ready, for the first glimpse of Operator 5. He shuffled on, smiling in his collar—and the smile was that of Jimmy Christopher...!

THE LEADERS of the besieged federal government were gathered in the Intelligence office at Baltimore known as sub-headquarters BM. Having fled from the Capital during the devastating storm that had established the enemy there, they had been called to these rooms by secret orders of the Chief Executive.

The President and Z-7 nodded doubt fully as Major-General Falk rumbled:

"Then it is agreed. It's a desperate measure which may hamstring our own defensive forces, but it's a gamble we must—"

149

The opening of the door interrupted. N-6, chief of the Baltimore area, entered with shining eyes. His blurted report brought exclamations of astonishment and eagerness from the President and Z-7.

"Operator 5 is here!"

They peered toward the door in puzzlement to see a grave-faced man quickly enter, wearing cleric's garb, whose face and bearing revealed no hint of resemblance to Operator 5; but when he spoke, his voice was Jimmy Christopher's.

Operator 5 smiled tightly as be took a towel which N-6 brought him. Wiping it across his face, he removed the color, and formations of plastic which he had used to change the contour of his features, and the face of Operator 5 appeared through the disguise.

"I was able to slip out of New York," he explained quickly, "by swimming the Hudson during the night. I disguised myself at NNJ in Newark. But I did not risk a message by wire because of the danger of WDC-13 listening in—and because the secret police of the enemy have crossed their frontiers in preparation for their master strategy."

"Is this," the Chief Executive asked tightly, "the information you are bringing us, Operator 5?"

"It is, Mr. President," Jimmy Christopher answered. "Briefly, it is this. The concentrations of the enemy will receive orders to expand their seized territories beginning at midnight tonight They will spread out from their key positions until all their lines meet. If their move succeeds, it will place them in complete control of every square inch of the United States."

"Midnight tonight?" Major-General Falk stared at the President "Operator 5, will they use their damnable cold projectors to cover their advances?"

"They no doubt will," Operator 5 replied, "but the advance will not take place until further orders signal it just prior to midnight tonight."

"THEN THERE is only one move we can make!" the Chief of Staff explained. "Mr. President we must carry through our plan to disrupt the enemy's lines of communication so that the final orders for the advance cannot reach the scattered positions of the invaders. Then, while their forces are still divided, we must throw the entire strength of our Army and Navy against their present positions."

"That, General Falk," Operator 5 announced firmly, "will insure disaster."

"What?" the Chief of Staff barked. "What do you mean?"

"We cannot allow the enemy to advance without a fight, Operator 5," the President objected in dismay.

Jimmy Christopher answered quickly: "Mr. President, the crisis we face forces us to use the most desperate tactics. We can no longer consider the safeguarding of our civilian non-combatants. We must attack all the strongholds of the enemy, and drive them out. Yet I insist that using all our infantry, all our Air Corps, all our naval guns, will bring us only defeat, as long as the neutron projectors remain to be turned against us. And I repeat, there is absolutely no way of physically destroying those damnable weapons."

"How, then—?" the Chief of Staff began.

"General Falk," Operator 5 countered, "you have mapped out a way of destroying the enemy's communicating system?"

"We have. We've learned that the invaders are using the telephone and telegraph systems they seized, as well as wireless. The cables, of course, run through territory which we still control. I have men stationed along every inch of the way. We have also prepared to use every broadcasting station in our territory to jam the air. At a given signal, every wire will be cut and the ether will be filled with such powerful disturbances that the wireless messages of the enemy will not be able to penetrate it. The move will isolate all the scattered points of invasion."

Operator 5 turned tensely. "Mr. President, Z-7, that move is an absolute necessity, dangerous as it is—but I urge that it be delayed until the last moment—until a few minutes before midnight tonight."

"What?" Falk barked. "And allow the enemy to flash their final signal for the advance? We haven't a moment to spare. We must destroy the invaders' communication systems right now!"

"To destroy them now," Operator 5 insisted, "would also destroy our last chance of victory."

The President asked anxiously. "Explain your meaning, Operator 5."

"CERTAINLY, SIR. The greatest strength of the invading forces lies in their neutron projectors. Their manpower is weaker than our own. Their use of submarines is limited to only a few of our cities. Their tank corps is strong, but ours is at least equal to it. They have not made use of air attacks because their own storms prohibit it, and because they are relying heavily on the cold effect. Thus, Mr. President, their chief power is their neutron projectors."

"But you have insisted from the start," Z-7 pointed out, "that there is no way of destroying the multiple defenses of the projectors."

Operator 5 continued quickly: "I have built up a plan. It's a terrific gamble. It may work—it may not. Yet as I see the situation, it's our only hope. It is to eliminate all the neutron projectors through a single command. Only one man can give that command—Commissar Kran. The neutron projectors must cease acting before the zero hour of midnight tonight, before the organized advance of the enemy begins—otherwise we can never hope to escape the invaders."

The Chief of Staff asked skeptically: "How do you propose to achieve that?"

"Allow me to explain only the essentials of my plan, Mr. President" Operator 5 rushed on, "because time is desperately short. It means that I must again penetrate past the enemy frontier into New York. I must reach Commissar Kran with the utmost dispatch if we are to stand the slightest chance of success. If you will grant me a free hand, Mr. President—?"

"Operator 5," the President answered, his eyes shining, "your own decisions are my orders!"

"Thank you, sir. Follow then, this plan of procedure. Flash orders to all men posted along the transcontinental wire systems, and to all broadcasting stations within our area, to go into action simultaneously at exactly midnight tonight. At that moment all the wires must be cut the ether must be jammed. At the zero hour all communication of any kind must cease. It will be strictly up to me to achieve my objective before the hour strikes. If I do not, we are doomed."

Operator 5 went on: "At the same time, flash orders to all our defense units, in accordance with your present plan, to attack all positions of the enemy. They must strike as powerfully as possible, not only to stem the enemy's advance, but to take the invaders' positions. It must be achieved at no matter what cost. Once the hour of midnight passes, victory will lie completely in the hands of the military, General Falk."

Jimmy Christopher glanced at the electric clock on the desk. "The rest is my job, sir. There isn't a moment to waste. The uniform belonging to Karle Kran—I must have it now. My credentials, also. My autogyro is to be fueled at once, and three men from this sub-headquarters are to be detailed under my orders. At the same time, orders must be flashed to the nearest army post to bring a blimp into action. The orders to the commander of that craft—"

OPERATOR 5'S eyes narrowed in thought. "He is to approach New York and time his flight so that he will be able to hover near the Vertex Building at exactly midnight. He must dip down into the city without power, to avoid arousing the enemy's anti-aircraft batteries. He is to drop rope-ladders as close to the mooring-mast as possible. He must use the utmost caution, for there are machine-guns mounted on every building surrounding the skyscraper, and if he is seen the craft will certainly be destroyed."

"I will relay your orders at once, Operator 5," Z-7 promised.

N-6 had brought to the desk the metallic uniform which had been stripped from Major Kran. He quickly inspected it, then took up the papers which had been removed from its pockets. One was an identification card bearing the scrawled signature of Commissar Kran. The other was a typed message which, Jimmy Christopher saw immediately, was crouched in the same code as the message he had found in the purse of Kada Aldee. He sat at the desk to translate it while he continued:

"Further, the timing of the blimp's flight must be absolutely exact. Because its motors cannot be used once it is over New York, it will not be able to maintain any position—it will be obliged to keep moving. The most important point is to have the craft in approximate position at midnight, where it will maneuver until a light-signal flashes from the mooring mast. It will then descend with rope-ladders lowered in an effort to pick up anyone who might be on the mast If that signal does not come—"

Jimmy Christopher's voice faded. "If it does not come immediately after midnight the craft must withdraw, for it will then have no mission to carry out."

Operator 5 intently studied the cipher message. He pieced letters together into words and read the few lines:

> Immediately following seizure of Washington Major Kran
> is to report to headquarters.—Commissar Kran.

It brought a glint to his eyes. Using the same system, he began the construction of another message. He worked intently, while Z-7 and N-6 relayed his orders; and when he completed the task, he folded the cryptic communication and placed it carefully in a secret pocket of his coat.

CHAPTER 11
COMMISSAR'S COMMAND

NIGHT BLANKETED Washington—and at the first darkening of the sky, a weird craft skirted high in the black zenith. Beneath it the Capital lay snow-piled, its streets lighted only by the flickering gleams of torches in the hands of the patrolling troops, and by the shine from the windows of governmental buildings which had been commandeered by the invaders. Enemy guns surveyed every strategic point; field pieces, submarines in the Potomac, massive tanks and anti-aircraft batteries strengthened the hold of the ruthless military machine. Washington, like New York, had become a stronghold of the raiders, where the devastating power of the cold threatened to descend at the first hint of counter-attack.

Wary of the raised snouts of the archie concentrations, the vaned craft circled under a minimum of power at the very limit of its ceiling. Three of the four men in it had parachute packs strapped to their backs; one steadied the controls as the others climbed over the cowling. They prepared to drop.

Operator 5 was the first to leap into cold space. The bell of the parachute which loomed above him was dyed black as a precaution against observation by the sentinels at the anti-aircraft batteries. As he floated downward, be heard the punging reports of two other 'chutes blossoming above him. Once the three were descending in the bitter air, the autogyro swerved and stole across the ceiling in the direction it had come.

Pulling the shroud-lines of their chutes, they directed themselves toward dark streets radiating from the capitol. Alertly they searched the canyons as they swept low. In accordance with the plan advanced by Jimmy Christopher, they navigated toward the snow-carpeted roof of a low building. Once they sank into the soft white, they spilled the wind from their chutes and shook off their harnesses.

As they crept down through a skylight, Operator 5 held the metallic uniform of Karle Kran bundled tightly under one arm. Above them, the gyro had vanished. Below them lay streets patrolled by armored killers. When they reached the pavement level, they made sure the way was clear, then darted out. Still following the maneuver outlined by Operator 5, they scattered.

Jimmy Christopher hurried past the corner to a door set below the level of the street. A key opened the way for him. He descended brick steps into a black passageway, lighting its length with an electric torch. He waited at a point where several tunnels met, while hurrying footfalls echoed. At his side came the two men who had come with him.

They had entered the underground recess by other doors, in order to avoid attracting attention; now they hurried with Jimmy Christopher toward the massive slab which had kept the raiders out. At the barred door of the brick cell, they turned their lights on the face of a man who stood gripping the iron bars and glowering. Karle Kran's eyes were a murderous fury as Operator 5 opened the door and stepped in.

A swift, sharp fight followed. The Commissar's son gave Operator 5 and his two men a stiff battle. The struggle ended when Jimmy Christopher's deft fingers shot home a jiu-jitsu blow which stiffened Kran's body. Temporarily paralyzed, the enemy officer toppled. Operator 5's two assistants carried him, rigid as a board, out of the cell and along the tunnel.

They followed the passage for long minutes, until Jimmy Christopher stopped at another door. Another key passed them through it. They mounted stairs, into a cavernous, black room. It was one of the secret garages maintained by the Intelligence in Washington. Operator 5 saw, to his relief, that it had escaped the scrutiny of the invaders. At his directions, his two comrades placed Kran in the rumble compartment of a heavy coupé while Operator 5 quickly drew on the mailed uniform.

He was transformed in a moment into a weird, glimmering figure whose darkened eyes peered at the two grim Intelligence men through protective goggles.

"This," he declared in a low tone, "is the end of your detail. Lacking uniforms, you can't attempt to pass out of the city with me. You must remain here. It means hunger, suffering, perhaps death—but there's no other way."

The two men smiled. "We knew that when we undertook the detail, Operator 5," one of them said. "It's all in the game. Good luck!"

Jimmy Christopher gripped their hands. Then he drew on his gloves, slipped behind the wheel of the coupé, and after a prolonged effort started the motor. The two Intelligence men opened a door for him as the car rolled. He turned into the narrow lane of the street, glanced back, and saw that the two men had imprisoned themselves. An erect, shining figure at the wheel, he sent the car rolling past patrolling troops and tanks.

Far on the north side of the city, he approached the barricade of the enemy. Guns bristled at him as he braked to a stop. Mailed officers approached; and Operator 5's heart beat heavily. With brisk, confident movements, he proffered the credentials of Major Kran, and the cipher message. Instantly the commander of the frontier guard snapped a salute.

"Pass on, Major Kran!"

ELEVEN O'CLOCK.... A heavy sedan turned upon the ramp of the Jersey terminus of the great George Washington Memorial Bridge, and sped up the slope. At the peak of the span, four massive tanks were in position, and their turret guns swung upon the car as it approached. Mailed troops fell into position at the weighty chain which barred the way, their rifles shouldered. A rod-backed officer in glimmering uniform strode to the car and gazed intently at the man in mail who sat at the wheel.

Peering at the proffered credentials, he blurted: "Major Kran! By all means, Major, pass on quickly! The Commissar has been very anxious to locate you!"

The heavy sedan spurted on, past the lowered chain, and again Operator 5 smiled tightly. He sped along Riverside Drive, following a cleared lane, and when he neared the barricaded section where the Vertex Building stood, he felt again a dull, pervading dread. He stepped from the car, proffered his credentials again.

"Pass in, Major!"

Mailed officers saluted him as he strode into the foyer of the skyscraper. Troops snapped to brisk attention as he passed. Alone in an elevator cab, he was lifted swiftly. Again he passed officers who wagged salutes as he entered the corridor of the headquarters offices. The adjutant advanced with stiff step to exclaim: "Major Kran! I will conduct you at once to the Commissar! He is overjoyed that you are safe. This way, Major!"

Operator 5 peered through the lenses of his hood, around the metal-paneled offices, and his gaze stopped on the face of an electric clock. Less than twenty-five minutes remained until the zero hour, when the striking of midnight would send a ruthless horde flooding over the United States. His pulse quickened with dread as he followed the adjutant through office after office—until, nearing the door which gave into the quarters of Commissar Kran, he stopped short.

As he peered, his heart went cold. In the adjutant's office a young woman, a man, and a boy were standing. Diane Elliot, disguised as Kada Aldee, gazed uncertainly at the mailed figure of Jimmy Christopher. John Christopher, white-faced, confronted him defiantly. Tim Donovan's eyes blazed. Operator 5 saw that the boy's hands and wrists were painfully swollen, that his ankles were lacerated, that his face was graven deep with lines of pain. The three gazed at Jimmy Christopher, but only Diane Elliot recognized the rich darkness of his eyes. She suppressed a start as he stood motionless.

The adjutant, opening the door of the Commissar's office, was stopped by Jimmy Christopher's disguised voice: "Wait! Adjutant, who are these prisoners?"

The captain smiled thinly. "The boy is one who has worked at the side of Operator 5 of the enemy Intelligence. We have, as you see, endeavored to induce him to give us information concerning Operator 5. He withstood the ordeal of the rack and would not speak. We have abandoned the attempt now that the zero hour is here. Commissar Kran is deciding the fate of the boy now. If you will follow me, Major—"

JIMMY CHRISTOPHER had turned to listen to voices speaking beyond the door of Kran's quarters. He heard an officer ask: "The order is to be executed at once, sir?"

The rumbling tones of the Commissar answered: "Yes. A firing squad for both the man and the boy. Enough of this! Where is my son?"

Again, as the adjutant began to open the connecting door, Operator 5 exclaimed: "One moment!" He saw terror in Diane Elliot's eyes, dread pictured on John Christopher's face, suffering on that of the staunch Irish lad. He said, with commanding firmness: "I desire the custody of these prisoners. They are to be remanded to me."

"It can be done, as you know, sir, only under the orders of the Commissar."

Operator 5 spun, simulating sudden fury. "Do you imagine that it will not be granted? Do you wish to be broken for your insolence? Would you like a taste of the firing squad yourself? I will personally obtain the permission. You are to consider these prisoners in my custody!"

The adjutant's face paled. "Very well, sir. The matter will be settled in a moment. May I suggest, Major, that inside these rooms, it is quite unnecessary to wear your hood and uniform?"

Jimmy Christopher's eyes glared through the goggles; he made no move to unmask. The connecting door opened; an officer strode out, and immediately the adjutant entered. Operator 5 heard the declaration: "Major Kran is here, sir!" He stepped close to Diane as a throaty answer followed: "My son! Bring him to me!" In a sharp whisper, Jimmy Christopher exclaimed:

"Diane—Tim—Dad! Go at once to the observation platform! Climb into the mooring mast if you can. Wait for me there! Do you hear me? Hurry!"

Ex-Operator Q-6 and the Irish lad stared in amazement at hearing the voice of Jimmy Christopher issue from the metal cowl. As they stood silent, Diane Elliot shook her head. "I won't go, Jimmy! Not without you! If you come—"

From behind Operator 5 came a snapping: "Major!"

He turned sharply, to see the adjutant standing in the doorway with eyes sharpened suspiciously. His heart grew cold under the intense scrutiny. He boldly strode close as the adjutant added:

"The Commissar grants you custody of the prisoners. Enter, Major."

"Escort them to the observation platform!"

"To—?"

"Do not question my orders!"

"Yes, sir!"

Operator 5 stepped to the sill of Commissar Kran's quarters. He realized that Diane Elliot was following. He shot a warning glance to the girl, but her chin lifted with defiant determination. When he stepped through the door and closed it, she followed. The huge Commissar Kran came heavily toward him, hands outstretched, his eyes shining with joy.

"My son! Karle!"

OPERATOR 5'S hand raised quickly toward his mask; but his hand poised as a sharp step sounded behind him. He stepped aside as the door opened and an officer appeared, eyes widened with alarm. Commissar Kran instantly made a violent, angry gesture of dismissal.

"Not now, captain! My son—"

"Commissar! One moment! An amazing report, received just this moment, from ZZ-64! He has found the home of our prisoner—the place intended to be used by the American Intelligence—and he declares that he found Kada Aldee held prisoner there!"

Jimmy Christopher stood rigid with dismay. Diane Elliot took one recoiling step, her hand raising in terror to her trembling lips. Commissar Kran glowered at the officer in bewilderment.

"What nonsense is this? Kada Aldee is here."

"ZZ-64 is Kada Aldee's brother, sir. There can be no possible mistake. This girl is an impostor! She is the one responsible for the leak of information from this headquarters, Commissar!"

Kran's voice thundered. "Then she is our prisoner! Hold her!"

The officer raised a hand to grip the arm of the appalled Diane Elliot. The metal-gloved fingers of Operator 5 clamped hard to his wrist and stayed the movement. Jimmy Christopher's eyes glared as he snapped:

"I will be responsible for her!"

The officer stood motionless; Commissar Kran scowled. The grumble of the commander's voice came. "If you wish, Karle. I have never refused you. But why—why do you keep your face masked?"

"That I will explain now!"

Operator 5 gestured sharply to the officer. As the mystified captain withdrew, Jimmy Christopher stepped to the door, closed it, and shot a bolt into its socket. He turned to face the huge Commissar. While Diane Elliot watched in despair, he deliberately raised his glimmering hands to his metal hood. With one quick movement he snatched it away.

Commissar Kran recoiled in dismay. He blurted: "You—you are not my son!"

"Your son, Commissar, is a prisoner of the United States Intelligence."

"What! Karle a prisoner? You—who are you?"

"I am Operator 5."

From Diane Elliot's numbed lips a whispered protest broke as Commissar Kran stared incredulously: "Jimmy—Jimmy, it's no use now!" The huge man's merciless eyes glinted with a triumphant light as he turned slowly to the desk. His hand moved, and stopped; and, peering back at Jimmy Christopher he spoke in a heavy whisper.

"Are you mad? Do you think that tricking me will gain you any advantage? Don't you realize that you are trapped here in this headquarters—both of you—and that you will be shot at once? Whatever your intention has been, Operator 5, you have lost. You *are* mad!"

Again the hand of Commissar Kran moved—toward a push-button on his desk.

"If you touch that button, Commissar," Operator 5 said quietly, "you will make yourself the murderer of your own son." The hand of the Commissar paused....

CHAPTER 12
ZERO HOUR

THE STEELY eyes of Kran turned piercingly on Operator 5. His blunt finger remained on the button; but it exerted no pressure. He did not move as Jimmy Christopher took slow steps forward.

"I realize. Commissar, that I've placed myself in a trap. I knew from the beginning that my deception must be revealed the moment I faced you here. My life is worth only a single command from you—I haven't allowed myself to hope that I'll ever leave this room alive. I've come here for only one purpose, Commissar."

Kran turned heavily. "Where is my son?" he demanded. "Tell me where he is!"

"If you wish to speak with him, Commissar, you have only to lift the receiver of your telephone. You have only to say, first, to your men at the exchanges: 'Connect me with Baltimore,' then:

'Connect me with BM.' Major Kran is waiting now to speak with you."

Uncertainty glimmered in the eyes of the Commissar; but he did not hesitate. He lifted the receiver. Ashy-faced, his great hands trembling, he growled into the transmitter the words which Operator 5 had directed him to utter:

"Connect me with Baltimore!"

Jimmy Christopher studied the whitened face of the supreme commander of the enemy forces. He knew this man to be a merciless and ruthless military genius. Human lives meant nothing to Commissar Kran—save the life of his only son. Operator 5 gambled as he pressed forward to whisper:

"Your son is a prisoner of war, Commissar. He faces the same fate you have inflicted upon hundreds of Americans. He has already been court-martialed. A sentence of death has been pronounced upon him, which is to be executed promptly at midnight tonight. You are about to speak to your son—perhaps for the last time. Do you hear me, Commissar?"

"Yes, yes!" Then, into the transmitter: "Connect me with BM!"

Operator 5 spoke rushingly while Diane Elliot watched his drawn face. "Only one man has the power to stay his execution—the President of the United States. He is there, at BM, with Major Kran, prepared to reprieve your son if I request it. Otherwise the sentence will be executed promptly on the stroke of midnight. Do you understand?"

Over the line Kran thundered: "Connect me with BM! Do you understand?"

"Time is pressing, Commissar," Opera tor 5 said quietly. "It is now only a matter of a few minutes until—"

Commissar Kran's great hands tightened on the instrument as he growled: "Major Kran! Call Major Kran to the telephone! At once!"

Operator 5 heard the answer of the prisoner speaking from BM in Baltimore: "Commissar! It is I—yes—Karle! Commissar—"

With a grueling effort, Kran controlled his overwhelming anxiety. "Karle! Is it true that you have been court-martialed? Is it true that only the President of the United States can save you?"

"It is true, Commissar, but—"

"It is set for midnight, Karle?"

"Midnight, Commissar. I implore you—"

"You are speaking freely? You are not being forced to say this?" THE VOICE on the line sharpened. "Freely—yes! Commissar, listen, I implore you! I am glad to give my life to the service of the cause. It is nothing compared with our great purpose! You must not forget that, Commissar!"

"Stay, Karle! Wait!" Kran rose from the instrument heavily, peering at Operator 5. "You have come here," he said huskily, "to bargain with me for the life of my son. What is it you demand?"

"Your order," Operator 5 answered promptly, "to flash this code message to the command at each of your scattered points of attack."

He proffered, as he spoke, the message he had written in the enemy's cipher at BM. The Commissar read its few lines at a glance. His eyes raised penetratingly to Operator 5's.

"You understand it fully?" Jimmy Christopher asked. "It is an order that the operation of every neutron projector shall immediately cease. It contains instructions to have the planned advance of your scattered units delayed until further orders."

Kran demanded slowly: "That is all?"

"That is all."

"And if I refuse?"

"The sentence of the court-martial upon your son will be carried out promptly at the stroke of midnight."

"And if I send these orders?"

"The President of the United States will grant your son a reprieve."

Shrewdly, his eyes glittering, the Commissar asked: "There are no other stipulations? Immediately these orders are flashed, you will request the President to reprieve my son? Once that is done, our bargain is completed?"

"Exactly, Commissar."

Kran smiled tightly.

He lowered the telephone. His eyes, as well as those of Operator 5, and Diane Elliot, turned toward the electric clock. Only four minutes remained until the stroke of midnight. With a tight smile, cold as the chill of his neutron projectors, the Commissar took up his pen.

"You must realize, Operator 5, that there is nothing in our bargain concerning the sparing of your own life—or of this girl. You will remain a prisoner here, even after these orders have been sent. You will, of course, suffer the penalty of death before the firing-squad."

Operator 5 answered tersely: "Midnight is nearing, Commissar. You will hurry, if you wish your son to live."

Grimly, Commissar Kran picked up his pen and scrawled on the cipher orders the signature necessary to their transmission. Immediately, his hard lips still curved, he strode into the room where the communications system centered.

Within these walls were the means of reaching every corner of the United States instantly by wireless, swiftly by wire—means of flashing orders to every area controlled by the raiders. An officer snapped to attention as Commissar Kran entered; and the huge man's first command was: "Maintain the connection with BM at Baltimore at all costs!"

He carried the cipher message to the chief-dispatcher and ordered: "To all units, at once!"

OPERATOR 5 peered at the electric clock in the room as the men at the switchboards went into action. Their voices became a guttural chorus above the click of cams and plugs as the hands of the dock passed the mark of one minute before midnight. Jimmy Christopher stood motionless, his heart racing, his blood cold, while the enemy command sent the message flashing through the ether toward the scattered points.

Only seconds remained until midnight when the action at the switchboards abruptly ceased. Commissar Kran turned with glaring eyes.

"The message has been transmitted. All neutron projectors have been ordered to cease operating. The zero hour of our advance has been held up. Confirmations from every point have come back."

"It is true, Commissar. You've kept your part of the bargain in good faith."

"Now it is time for you to keep yours!"

A fierce sense of triumph filled Operator 5 as he strode briskly toward the Commissar's quarters. He had achieved his desperate purpose. He knew that the shrewd mind of Commissar Kran was even now framing a plan to nullify his triumph; but he grimly strode to the telephone on the commander's deck. He spoke crisply: "Operator 5 calling!"

"Z-7 on the wire!"

"The orders have been sent The President must reprieve Major Kran at once!"

Instantly the huge hand of Commissar Kran tore the instrument from Operator 5's fingers. The commander heard the clicking sounds of the breaking connections. He roared into the transmitter: "Guard the line to Baltimore! It must not be used again except by me!"

He lowered the telephone and his eyes gleamed triumphantly. "Now you will not be able to countermand the reprieve—but our bargain does not bind me against countermanding the orders you forced me to send!"

Quietly Operator 5 asked: "Do you intend to countermand them, Commissar?"

Kran was stabbing his blunt fingers at the buttons on his desk. Officers rushed to his side in response. He scribbled rapidly on a heavy page of paper as they approached, and scrawled his signature. He gave it to the adjutant, snarled:

"Countermand my latest orders! Neutron projectors at all

points are to operate according to plan! The advance is to begin at once! Our master strategy holds! Flash every area instantly by radio and have the confirmations relayed to me at once!"

The dismayed officers sped toward the door of the communications-room. Operator 5 peered at the hard-faced Kran and smiled tightly. His hand sought Diane Elliot's and closed hotly on it He said in a rush:

"My compliments, Commissar!"

HE TURNED quickly, urging Diane ahead of him. Kran's icy eyes followed their move with contempt. He followed with quick, heavy steps, an order rising to his lips: "Hold Operator 5 and the girl—execute them at once!" But as he was about to speak the words, four officers rushed into the room through another door, their faces white with consternation, dismay reflected in their eyes.

"The air is jammed, Commissar!" "Wireless transmission has become impossible!" "The telephone wires are dead!" "The telegraph is no longer working!" "We are unable to flash the countermand, sir!" "Your orders crippling the projectors and delaying the advance were the last to go through, sir!" "No countermand, Commissar—no countermand!"

Commissar Kran stared for one stunned moment, then his thundering officers sprang to the corridor doors with drawn guns. As they hurried toward the doors of the fire-stairs, they heard the roaring storm of the Commissar's voice:

"Kill them! Kill them! Kill them!"

Jimmy Christopher and Diane Elliot had sped out the headquarters offices to those stairs. They had bounded up two flights, quickly, into another corridor. There, in answer to a breathless question, the girl had blurted: "In those rooms—yes!" Now Operator 5 sped to the nearest door. He heard beyond it a subdued sputtering; he felt a prickling of his scalp and sensed the pungency of ozone as he twisted frantically at the knob. He found the way barred, and desperately he drove the butt of his automatic against the glass pane.

His hand, thrust in, drew a bolt and he stepped into a big room in which he glimpsed a score of men working at monstrous, grotesque devices. Pointing toward the walls, glowing with an iridescent light, were gigantic quartz tubes in which cathodes and anodes were sparkling white hot. They were directed at all angles, so that the spreading beams of the cold-force enveloped all the city. Jimmy Christopher's eyes flashed swiftly from tube to tube as he leveled his automatic and fired.

Swiftly, with devastating effect, his bullets crashed into the tubes. Glass shattered under the impacts, the broken vacuums produced deafening explosions as stinging hot fragments flew. Fire shot up as Operator 5's bullets sent destruction into one after another of the neutron projectors. As streaming flame mingled with muffled explosions, he whirled blindly out the door.

Steps were ringing on the stairs as he thrust Diane Elliot toward them. He whipped the clip from his weapon and inserted another, brought from a pocket of the mailed uniform, as he rushed after her. He turned his automatic upon the officers rushing up the steps and it blazed defiance. Their guns echoed a challenge; and Operator 5 felt the impact of bullets against the metal scales of his garment as he sped upward. He fired as he mounted, and with Diane Elliot, whirled onto the observation platform of the building.

A third clip was ready in his gun as he raced toward the man and the boy standing on the platform. Operator 5's commands, as Karle Kran, had brought them here in the company of two officers. The men in uniform stared as Jimmy Christopher covered them and commanded: "Tim, Dad—into the mooring-mast—quick! Go with them, Di!"

HIS AUTOMATIC spat again as the officers dragged at their holstered automatics. They slipped away while Operator 5 stood backed to the door. It jarred, as the pursuing officers threw their weight against it. Twice more, in swift succession he sent slugs whistling toward the men on the platform, driving one back with broken gun-arm, and sending the other spilling to the floor. He whirled, backed from the door, fired through it swiftly when it began to open. Then, when it slapped shut upon cries of pain and rage, he spun to enter the mooring-mast.

Above him, Tim Donovan and John Christopher were clinging to the narrow stairs, hurrying Diane Elliot between them. Jimmy Christopher peered around through the gleaming latticework of the mask as he dashed up. He saw, at first, only empty sky. A pang of despair pinched his heart—fear that his carefully laid plans had gone awry. But as he climbed he heard a storm breaking—the storm of battle roaring along the western front of Manhattan.

Gun-fire burst over the river; rifles were blasting on the bridge; the thunder of airplanes was sweeping through the sky.

Operator 5's bullets sent destruction into one after another of the diabolical devices!

Searchlights stabbed upward as anti-aircraft batteries went into action. The snarling of enemy tanks became a deafening din rising from the canyons of the city. The holocaust of armed conflict thundered ever more loudly as Operator 5 reached the mooring-mast and, with hand gripped hard on an electric torch, flashed a signal into the sky.

He saw it then—a black cloud which swung rapidly closer. "Catch the ladders!" he urged. "It's your only chance!"

He saw them dangling from the gondola of the blimp as it loomed closer—rope ladders whipping in the night wind. Operator 5 turned again to the narrow stairway which led to the peak of the mast. Footfalls ringing below meant that the officers were still following. He leveled his automatic and sent slugs rattling downward.

He backed as John Christopher opened the gate upon empty space. The silent craft was swinging still closer, its ladders dangling. Tim Donovan gripped a railing and reached far out as one whipped close. He groped for it, missed; and on his second try, his hard hand closed tightly. "Di!" he urged, and instantly he forced the girl to seize the support.

He clung frantically, closing his arms around Diane, and felt the powerful lift that took him from the platform. Operator 5 gripped the arm of John Christopher as a second of the ladders swung near. Together they grasped it and clung. They clutched the rungs desperately as the mooring-mast swung away from them—as uniformed men appeared on the platform with guns spitting.

Operator 5 urged John Christopher to climb; and he saw Tim

Donovan clinging to the end of the other ladder while Diane Elliot drew herself upward. The blimp became lost in the blackness as Jimmy Christopher climbed....

He pulled himself in as its power plant roared and it propellers bit into the air. Breathless, he turned to Diane Elliot; his swift glance showed that she was unhurt. She flung her arms around him and clung as she sobbed in a paroxysm of relief. Tim Donovan peered up and grinned; John Christopher stood stunned.

"You're all right, Di—you're all right!" Operator 5 urged reassuringly. "You did it like a good soldier—it wouldn't have been possible without you. We're out of it now—do you understand? Di."

The girl could only cling to Operator 5 and sob over and over: "Jimmy!"

Tim Donovan forgot the pain of the torture he had suffered as he grinned at Operator 5. "Gee, Jimmy! You got us clear! What's happening down there, Jimmy?"

Operator 5 peered down at the dark band of the Hudson. It had become the frontier of a savage battle. The great bridge was marked by flashing gun-fire. The flare of dropping bombs were blinding geysers in the river, driving toward the lurking submarines. Far out on the bay, great battleships were hurling projectiles toward the line of conflict. The anti-aircraft batteries of the invaders were storming against the swooping wings of U.S. battle squadrons. The terrific counter-attack sounded across the Hudson.

The United States defenses had struck—and while they advanced, the cold began to disappear....

HISTORY NEVER recorded a battle to compare with the second siege of New York. It raged throughout the night, while massing United States Infantry poured over the giant span and through the under-river tunnels; while projectiles and bombs burst open the way for the advance; while tanks clashed with tanks and mailed men retreated. When the light of dawn broke over the battle-scarred city, the United States army and navy were the commanding power in the metropolis.

Into headquarters BM, reports flashed by wireless through air no longer jammed.

...BM... SPECIAL... SAN FRANCISCO RETAKEN... INVADERS DRIVEN FROM CHICAGO... PANAMA CANAL ZONE REPORTS COMPLETE VICTORY FOR U.S. FORCES... BOSTON RECLAIMED... MISSISSIPPI REOPENED WITH SALVATION OF NEW ORLEANS... RAIDERS ROUTED FROM ST. LOUIS....

Reports from the field of battle, added to a dispatch which flashed from the stronghold that once had been the headquarters of the enemy invasion:

...BM... SPECIAL... COMMISSAR KRAN COMMITTED SUICIDE IN HIS HEADQUARTERS UPON RECEIVING NEWS OF HIS DEFEAT... VB-NY....

OVER THE highway leading into Washington, D.C., a parade of swift cars sped. They passed barricades which had been erected by the raiders, but now were posted with United States marines. They wound deep into a city from which the ravages of winter were passing. Once they turned down Pennsylvania Avenue, one swung into the grounds of the White House from which the mailed troopers had been driven. Others scattered to the government buildings around the hub of the Capital. The last proceeded alone toward an edifice which had been erected for the purpose of housing international delegations.

When it paused, Operator 5 stepped from it, followed by Z-7. They mounted the steps, followed by a number of Intelligence operators. They were acting upon a mission set for them by the receipt of the first message from the Washington area:

> ... BM... SPECIAL... CONFERENCE OF FOREIGN EMISSARIES IN PAN-NATIONAL HALL GATHER-ING NOW... PURPOSE BELIEVED TO BE RECOG-NITION OF IPSO FACTO GOVERNMENT... IMMEDIATE ACTION IMPERATIVE... WDC-T....

IN THE conference room of that great building, around the very table at which the repudiated Pan-National Treaty had been signed, the representatives of every great world power had gathered. They faced each other solemnly, listening to the man at the head of the table.

"The very lack of news, gentlemen, indicates victory for the invading forces. The passing of the cold means that it is no longer necessary for the subjugation of the United States. The government of the United States no longer exists. We have no alternative but to recognize the new government which has arisen in its place. Of course, gentlemen, there is some slight possibility that I am mistaken, but of course—"

"You are quite mistaken!"

THE VOICE rang clearly from the door which had quietly opened in the conference room. The eyes of the ambassadors turned startled upon Jimmy Christopher as he strode forward. Z-7 followed Operator 5 to the head of the table. Behind them the Intelligence agents spread with leveled guns. There was no word spoken while Operator 5 gazed with a grim smile at the representatives.

"Gentlemen, it is not the government of the United States which no longer exists—it is the invading force which has been wiped out. Every city seized by the raiders has been reclaimed. At this very moment, gentlemen, the President of the United States is broadcasting from the White House a reassuring message to the people of the nation."

The representatives stared aghast.

"Yours," Operator 5 continued grimly, "has been the most staggering act of hypocrisy in the history of the world. You will, gentlemen, consider yourselves the prisoners of the United States Intelligence. For—"

Jimmy Christopher's smile grew tighter, and the deep blue of his eyes brightened: "Your cause is forever lost."

POPULAR HERO PULPS AVAILABLE NOW:

THE SECRET 6

- ❏ #1: The Red Shadow $13.95
- ❏ #2: House of Walking Corpses $13.95
- ❏ #3: The Monster Murders $13.95
- ❏ #4: The Golden Alligator $13.95

CAPTAIN ZERO

- ❏ #1: City of Deadly Sleep $13.95
- ❏ #2: The Mark of Zero! $13.95
- ❏ #3: The Golden Murder Syndicate $13.95

OPERATOR 5

- ❏ #1: The Masked Invasion $13.95
- ❏ #2: The Invisible Empire $13.95
- ❏ #3: The Yellow Scourge $13.95
- ❏ #4: The Melting Death $13.95
- ❏ #5: Cavern of the Damned $13.95
- ❏ #6: Master of Broken Men $13.95
- ❏ #7: Invasion of the Dark Legions $13.95
- ❏ #8: The Green Death Mists $13.95
- ❏ #9: Legions of Starvation $13.95
- ❏ #10: The Red Invader $13.95
- ❏ #11: The League of War-Monsters $13.95
- ❏ #12: The Army of the Dead $13.95
- ❏ #13: March of the Flame Marauders $13.95
- ❏ #14: Blood Reign of the Dictator $13.95
- ❏ #15: Invasion of the Yellow Warlords $13.95
- ❏ #16: Legions of the Death Master $13.95
- ❏ #17: Hosts of the Flaming Death $13.95
- ❏ #18: Invasion of the Crimson Death Cult $13.95
- ❏ **NEW:** #19: Attack of the Blizzard Men $13.95

DUSTY AYRES AND HIS BATTLE BIRDS

- ❏ #1: Black Lightning! $13.95
- ❏ #2: Crimson Doom $13.95
- ❏ #3: The Purple Tornado $13.95
- ❏ #4: The Screaming Eye $13.95
- ❏ #5: The Green Thunderbolt $13.95
- ❏ #6: The Red Destroyer $13.95
- ❏ #7: The White Death $13.95
- ❏ #8: The Black Avenger $13.95
- ❏ #9: The Silver Typhoon $13.95
- ❏ #10: The Troposphere F-S $13.95
- ❏ #11: The Blue Cyclone $13.95
- ❏ #12: The Tesla Raiders $13.95

MAVERICKS

- ❏ #1: Five Against the Law $12.95
- ❏ #2: Mesquite Manhunters $12.95
- ❏ #3: Bait for the Lobo Pack $12.95
- ❏ #4: Doc Grimson's Outlaw Posse $12.95
- ❏ #5: Charlie Parr's Gunsmoke Cure $12.95